* * * * * * *

"Sorry that we had to call you out on this one after last week, Nick," Jerry said, knowing what my last case had been like.

"That's okay. What do we have here?"

"We have the body of a young woman. That young fellow over there claims to have discovered the body in the water and pulled it out of the lake."

"You sound like you don't believe him," I said as I glanced over at the young man Jerry had pointed out.

"Let's just say, I have some serious doubts. I'll be able to tell you more by tomorrow."

I noticed that the young man was being questioned by Lieutenant John Brooks, a detective from another precinct who seemed to show up in the most unlikely places.

"What's he doing here? Isn't he working out of West Park Division?"

"I guess," Jerry said as he shrugged and then continued.

I turned my attention back to Jerry and listened to him. I could worry about Brooks later.

* * * * * * *

Other titles by J.E. Terrall

Western Short Stories
  The Old West
  The Frontier
  Untamed Land
  Tales From the Territory

Western Novels
  Conflict in Elkhorn Valley
  Lazy A Ranch
    (A Modern Western)

Romance Novels
  Balboa Rendezvous
  Sing for Me
  Return to Me
  Forever Yours

Mystery/Suspense/Thriller
  I Can See Clearly
  The Return Home
  The Inheritance

Nick McCord Mysteries
  Vol – 1 Murder at Gill's Point
  Vol – 2 Death of a Flower
  Vol – 3 A Dead Man's Treasure
  Vol – 4 Blackjack, A Game to Die For
  Vol – 5 Death on the Lakes
  Vol – 6 Secrets Can Get You Killed

Peter Blackstone Mysteries
  Murder in the Foothills
  Murder on the Crystal Blue
  Murder of My Love

Frank Tidsdale Mysteries
  Death by Design

DEATH OF A FLOWER

**A Nick McCord Mystery
by
J. E. Terrall**

ISBN: 978-0-9844591-9-3

This is a work of fiction. Names, characters, and incidents are either a product of the author's imagination or are used fictitiously, and any resemblance to actual persons, living or dead, is purely coincidental.

Printed in the United States of America
First and Second Printing / 2009   www.lulu.com
Third printing / 2014   www.creatspace.com

Cover: Front cover designed by Phyllis Terrall

Book Layout/
Formatting: J.E. Terrall
               Custer, South Dakota

DEATH OF A FLOWER

A Nick McCord Mystery

To David

CHAPTER ONE

It was a quiet summer afternoon in Milwaukee. The air was still and there wasn't a cloud in the sky. About all anyone could say about the weather was that it was hot. It was a much better day to be at the beach than to be cooped up in an office behind a desk stacked high with papers. But that was where I could be found, at least for the moment.

I had just finished typing the final pages of a report on a case that I had been working on for what seemed like a very long time. As I was attaching one of the police photos to my report, I couldn't help taking one last look at it. It was a photo of a young woman who had been raped and beaten to death. My heart went out to the parents of the young victim of another senseless crime. The fact that her killer had been shot to death by a police officer when he tried to escape did nothing to make me feel better. The young woman was dead and there was nothing that could possibly fill the void in her family left by her death. Her parents would miss her forever.

I laid the photos down on top of my report and let out a sigh of relief that I could finally put this one to rest. Although this case could now be closed, it was far from the end of such violence. It left me wondering what was happening to our society. There was no doubt in my mind that there would be another case, just as tragic and just as senseless, waiting for me as soon as I filed this one away.

I picked up the police reports, the autopsy report along with the lab reports and the photos, and slipped them into an official looking envelope. After sealing it, I scribbled a short note on the outside of the envelope and dropped the envelope into the "out" basket on the corner of my desk. There, it was over, I thought to myself. But the envelope no more than hit the tray when the phone began to ring sending a chill down my spine.

"Detective McCord, may I help you?"

"Nick, this is Joe. There's a body that's been pulled out of the lake at South Shore Park. I want you to get down there as quick as you can. It looks like murder."

"What makes you think its murder, Captain?"

"A bullet hole in the base of the victim's skull," he replied without emotion.

"I'm on my way," I said and hung up the phone.

The old saying that there is no rest for the wicked came to mind as I grabbed my sport coat off the back of the chair, and started out of the office. I left the police garage and drove to South Shore Park.

South Shore Park is located at the southern edge of Milwaukee along the Lake Michigan shoreline. It was once a popular place for families to spend their summer afternoons. However, in recent years there had been a few problems with drug dealers and gangs using the park as a place to meet. For obvious reasons, not as many families were going to the park anymore.

It took me a good twenty minutes to get to the park from the office. Once I arrived, it was easy to find where the body had been found. A large group of people had gathered around the bright yellow tape that cordoned off part of the beach to only the authorities. Typical of most large cities, and small ones, too, I guess, a dead body lying around tends to draw a crowd.

I had to push my way through the crowd just to get to the yellow tape that surrounded the crime scene. I no more then slipped under the yellow tape when I found myself standing face to face with a rather large police officer that didn't look to be very friendly. It was clear that he had just about had it with the crowd pushing and shoving in order to get a better look at what was going on. Morbid curiosity, I guess.

"Detective McCord," I said as I flashed my badge and ID card.

He hesitated only a second to glance at the badge before stepping aside and letting me pass.

"Hi, Jerry, what's up?" I asked as I approached the body that was covered with a white sheet.

Jerry Kowalski was a short balding man in his late forties. He wore glasses that sort of sat on the end of his nose making him look very much like the absent-minded professor. The big difference was that Jerry didn't forget anything. He was a man who paid close attention to detail, every little detail. Very little slipped by him, but that was as it should be because he was the Medical Examiner.

"Sorry that we had to call you out on this one after last week," he said, knowing what my last case had been like.

"That's okay. What do we have here?"

"We have the body of a young woman. That young fellow over there claims to have discovered the body in the water and pulled it out of the lake."

"You sound like you don't believe him," I said as I glanced over at the young man Jerry had pointed out.

"Let's just say, I have some serious doubts. I'll be able to tell you more by tomorrow."

I noticed that the young man was being questioned by Lieutenant John Brooks, a detective from another precinct who seemed to show up in the most unlikely places.

"What's he doing here? Isn't he working out of West Park Division?"

"I guess," Jerry said as he shrugged and then continued.

I turned my attention back to Jerry and listened to him. I could worry about Brooks later.

"The woman is in her early to mid twenties, my best guess is about twenty-one, maybe twenty-two. It's hard to tell these days.

"She has a single bullet hole from a small caliber weapon, probably a .22 or .25 caliber pistol, in the back of her head at the base of the skull. I'll be able to tell you what caliber later.

"She was shot at very close range. There are powder burns in her hair and on the skin. There is no exit wound as far as I can tell. It would be my guess that the bullet probably bounced around inside her head and is still there. This one has all the earmarks of an execution style killing.

"She's been in the water, but I doubt for very long. Maybe, long enough to get her clothes wet, but not much longer then that. At least that's my best guess right now. I'll be able to tell you more about her after I complete an autopsy."

"Can you tell me her name and where she lived?"

"Come on, Nick. I'm good at my job, but not that good. She doesn't have any ID on her. We haven't found a purse or wallet so far. That would indicate that she wasn't killed here. There are no labels in her clothes, not even the brand labels. Her clothes are fairly expensive, that much I can tell you. It's all yours now."

"No labels on her clothes?" I asked.

"None," he replied.

"Thanks, Jerry," I said as I knelt down and lifted the sheet up to look at the body.

The victim had been a very nice looking woman with her whole life still ahead of her, but someone had snuffed it out as calmly as you would blow out a candle. I had to wonder what sort of person would do that to someone so beautiful? I also had to wonder what kind of people had she gotten involved with that could do this sort of thing?

"Jerry, look here. What caused the red marks on her face?"

"Not sure. Could be from almost anything. It could have happened during a struggle or it could have been caused by a slap on the face by someone wearing a big ring. It's hard to tell."

"Let me know what you find out as soon as you can."

"Sure."

As I dropped the sheet back over the girl's face and stood up, I looked toward Lieutenant Brooks who was standing off away from the people gathered on the beach. He was still questioning the young man who was supposed to have discovered the body. It seemed to me that there was something odd about what was going on between them. Although I couldn't hear what was being said, Brooks didn't appear to be questioning the young man. It looked more like they were having a casual conversation much like one would have with a friend or an acquaintance.

On second thought, it was more like Brooks was giving the young man instructions, but instructions on what? I got the distinct impression that Brooks knew the young man, and probably had known him for some time.

Lieutenant Brooks looked toward me and we made eye contact for several seconds, during which time Brooks stopped talking to the young man. I got the feeling that he had to force himself to turn away in order to resume his conversation.

Several questions began to form in my mind. Questions like, what was Brooks doing in this part of town? What was his interest in this case? And who was the young man he was talking to?

Captain Joe Sinclair had clearly assigned this case to me. After all it was in our precinct. I was not going to have anyone, especially Lieutenant Brooks, interfere with my investigation.

As I started across the beach, my thoughts turned to Brooks. It was not the first time that Lieutenant Brooks and I had crossed paths. Several years ago I had been working on a big drug case. It had taken me the better part of a year to put it together. Shortly before I was ready to spring my trap and start making arrests, I suddenly found myself working with Brooks. I was never able to figure out how he got put on the case with me, especially since I was so close to wrapping it up, but it happened.

After months of long, hard work, I had been able to uncover enough solid evidence on one of the local crime bosses that I was sure it would hold up in court. There was no doubt in my mind that I could put the maggot away for the rest of his life. But within days of Brooks's arrival on the scene, the most important single piece of evidence suddenly disappeared. The evidence would have sent Frank Angelini away for a long time. But without it, there was not a chance of convicting Angelini of anything, not even for J-walking.

I was never able to prove anything, but I was convinced that Lieutenant Brooks had something to do with the disappearance of the evidence. During my investigation of Frank Angelini, little bits of information seemed to crop up here and there that pointed to a connection between Brooks and the Angelini family. It was common knowledge that Brooks had gone to college with Frank Angelini's younger brother, but I had nothing solid to connect the two of them together other than the fact that they would certainly have known each other.

"Well, if it isn't the great Detective Nicholas McCord," Brooks said with a big sarcastic grin on his face as I approached him.

"What are you doing around here? I thought you belonged over at West Park Division."

"I just thought I'd stop by and give you a hand."

"I sure as hell don't need any of your kind of help."

"Now, just a minute," Brooks responded with a note of anger.

"No, you wait a minute. The last time you helped me, I lost the case and your friend Frank Angelini got off scot-free."

"It's not my fault that you can't put a case together that you can make stick," he said with a grin.

"You son of a..."

I was suddenly interrupted by a voice from behind me.

"All right, you two. Knock it off and get to work."

I turned around to find Captain Sinclair coming toward us. It was clear by the look on his face that he was not one bit happy to find two detectives arguing in front of fellow officers, and especially so close to a couple of members of the press who were trying to get whatever information they could for the evening news.

"What are you doing here?" Captain Sinclair asked Lieutenant Brooks. "You're a little out of your territory, aren't you?"

"I was in the area when the call came in. I decided to stop by and see if I could help."

"I sure as hell don't need his kind of help," I stated flatly. "Who you covering up for this time?"

"I resent that," Lieutenant Brooks said as he stepped toward me.

There was no doubt that my last comment had hit a nerve and had made Brooks angry. I was almost hoping that he would take a swing at me. It would give me the excuse I needed to knock him on his butt.

"That's enough. McCord, take over here. As for you, Brooks, you get back to your own precinct, and now," Captain Sinclair ordered sharply.

"Okay. By the way, the kid doesn't know anything," Lieutenant Brooks said before he turned and started off across the beach toward the parking lot.

"I'm sure you won't mind if I question him myself," I said as I walked past Brooks toward the young man.

Needless to say I didn't trust anything Brooks said or did. I needed to find out what this young man knew, but more importantly, I wanted to know who he was and who his friends might be.

As I walked toward the young man, I glanced back to see Brooks watching me. Actually it was more like glaring at me. My first thought was that he was just angry because I had made it clear that I didn't like him or trust him. But as I looked back at the young man, I caught him looking at Brooks as if he was looking for some clue as to what he should say to me.

Maybe, I'm getting a little paranoid. After all, I had no reason to believe that the young man had anything to do with anything except discovering the body. This was no time to let my dislike and lack of trust of Lieutenant Brooks get in the way of my better judgment, or in the way of doing good police work.

"Hi," I said to the young man.

"Hi," he replied cautiously.

The young man looked like he might be afraid to talk to me alone. Now that struck me as strange since he didn't seem to have any problem talking to Brooks. It crossed my mind again that the two of them probably knew each other before today.

"I'm Detective McCord. I'd like to ask you a few questions."

"Sure, but I told Lieutenant Brooks everything I know," the young man said nervously.

"That's good, but Lieutenant Brooks had to leave and I didn't get a chance to talk to him very much."

The young man seemed rather tense and keyed up. I noticed that he kept looking in the direction Brooks had taken. When I glanced over my shoulder to see what he found so interesting, I saw Brooks sitting in his car watching us. I found it interesting that Brooks had not left the area, especially since he had been ordered to do so.

When Brooks saw me looking in his direction, he started his car and quickly drove away. Something about it didn't set well with me. If he had just stopped to help, why was he so interested in the young man talking to me? Why didn't he just leave? There was no doubt in my mind that Brooks had plenty to do in his own precinct without interfering in my investigation. The more I thought about it, "concerned" seemed to be a more appropriate way of describing Brooks's interest in what I was doing.

As I turned back toward the young man, I noticed that he seemed almost preoccupied with watching Brooks drive away. The look on his face was that of someone who had just been left to fend for himself. He had been deserted without any clear directions on what to say or what to do.

"What's your name?"

The suddenness of my question seemed to startle the young man. He looked confused as if he had not heard my question.

"What's your name?" I asked again.

"Jonathan Ehman," he replied nervously.

"What were you doing here in the park?"

"I was just out for a walk."

"Just walking?"

"Yeah. It's a nice day."

"Where do you live, Jonathan? By the way, you know it won't take me long to find out."

I watched him closely for a reaction. He looked at me, then down at his shoes. He pushed a little sand around with his foot, making small circles in the sand. It took him a moment or two before he looked up to answer.

"I live on Fifty-second Street, off Wright."

It didn't take a genius to figure out that he was not here just for a walk. The location he gave me was clear across town, several miles away. I found it very hard to believe that he was the type to walk for exercise, let alone walk so far from home without a very good reason.

"Tell me what you saw, Jonathan."

"I was walking along the beach and saw the girl floating in the water. I dragged her up on the beach and called the cops, - ah - the police," he said as he shifted his weight from one leg to the other.

"That's it?"

"Yeah, that's it."

"She wasn't already on the beach?"

He looked surprised at my question. It took him a moment or two to decide just what to say.

"No. I pulled her out of the water."

I had dealt with young punks like him for years. That was probably all I was going to get out of him for now. I could see no need to waste any more time with him. I needed to find out more about him before I talked to him again. Maybe there was something in his background that I could use as leverage to get to the truth.

"Okay, you can go. I'll be in touch with you, later."

He looked at me as if he had expected me to drill him for hours. It was a complete surprise to him that I was going to let him walk. It caught him off guard.

"That's it?" he asked.

"I'll get hold of Lieutenant Brooks and talk with him. I'm sure you told him the same thing you told me."

"Yeah, I did."

Jonathan seemed very much relieved that he was free to go. As he turned and walked away, I glanced down at his shoes and the bottoms of his pant legs. It was easy to see that he had not been wading in the water. His shoes and pants were dry. He might have kicked off his shoes, but I doubted that he would have taken the time to roll up his pants before wading into the lake to pull the body up on shore.

I watched him for a little while. There was something about what he had said that gnawed at me, something that didn't seem to want to register in my head. It had nothing to do with the fact that his shoes and pants were dry.

Suddenly it hit me. This young man lived on Fifty-second Street near Wright, which would put him in the West Park Division. That was Lieutenant Brooks's precinct. From the way Jonathan had acted earlier, my guess was that Brooks knew him. What did that prove? I knew that I was using a pretty thin thread to connect the two of them together. But I had no intentions of letting go of that particular thread until I had a chance to check it out.

I took a minute to look around. All the people that were in the park when the police first arrived had been questioned. The officers at the scene had taken names and addresses of possible witnesses. Their statements of what they had seen and heard had been taken down. The body had already been removed and taken downtown for an autopsy.

So far nothing had been found on her that would help to identify her. It could take a day or two, even longer, before I might find out who the girl was, and longer to find out how she got here.

There was nothing more that could be done here. Curiosity seekers had trampled any evidence that might have been left in the sand. The way the body had been found and the condition of her clothes indicated that the beach was not the primary crime scene, only the place where the body had been dumped.

It was time to go back downtown and sort through the information that had been gathered. I needed to see if I could come up with anything that might give me some direction. What I really needed was a clue as to what really happened, and to who had killed this young woman.

CHAPTER TWO

I returned to the office and began going over the names and addresses of the people who had been in the park when the young woman's body was found. Since it had taken several officers to interview everyone in the park, I had several lists to go over. At my first run through the lists, I didn't recognize most the names. However, there were a couple of names that were familiar, other than Ehman's. The rest of the names and addresses were from all over the city and didn't mean anything to me.

Of the two names that I did immediately recognize, the first was that of Danny Minger. Danny was a tall, skinny kid with long dark brown hair. He looked as if a light breeze would blow him over. Danny was a thief and drug pusher who had an arrest record as long as his arm, but all small time stuff. I had dealt with him a time or two in the past. He wasn't very bright and he was afraid of his own shadow. Every time he was picked up for questioning, he would talk as if his life depended on it.

The problem I had was that I couldn't picture him having anything to do with murder. It was not likely that Danny could kill anyone, especially with a gun at close range. He had always been afraid of guns. Selling a few drugs, stealing a wallet or a watch was more his style, but not murder.

The second name I recognized was Charley Mitken. Now Charley was a completely different story. He stood over six feet tall, had broad shoulders and a barrel chest. There was never any doubt that he was a strong man. He was tough and he was as mean as they come. He was also known for using a .45 caliber semi-automatic pistol as his weapon of choice, the kind that would blow a person's head completely off. The gun used in the murder of the girl would not have been the type of gun Charley would have used. He liked to make a statement when he acted against someone.

I had had several run-ins with Charley over the past few years. He was a hard man to deal with. The one thing that you could be certain of was that he would fight you every inch of the way. I even had him jailed for resisting arrest once. He had been arrested a number of times on suspicion of murder, assault, extortion and numerous other felonies. On one occasion, he was accused of beating a man to death with the man's own baseball bat just because he didn't like the guy's choice of baseball teams.

With all that Charley had been arrested for, he was never convicted of any charge more serious than misdemeanor assault. There were two reasons for that. One was he always had a very good lawyer. The other was that it seemed that every time he was arrested and booked on a serious charge, the witnesses would suddenly disappear or couldn't remember seeing anything. In a couple of cases, the witnesses simply failed to show up in court at the appointed time. Their bodies were found later in some lonely place like a woods or a field outside the city.

In Charley's case, he could kill someone without batting an eyelid, but he usually did it in a more brutal, more violent way. And although he was known to use a gun on occasion, he preferred to beat his victim with a club or with his bare hands just because he could. This execution style of murder was not his style.

I had two completely different types of criminals who were in the same area where a murder victim had been found. Yet neither of them fit the profile of the kind of person who would commit an execution style murder. It looked more like a mob hit to me, or it had been made to look like a mob hit.

A quick check of Danny's and Charley's last known addresses showed me that neither one of them lived anywhere near South Shore Park. My most haunting questions at the moment were, what were those two doing at South Shore Park, and what was the connection between them?

The more I thought about it, the more I wondered if there was any connection between Danny and Charley at all. Unless one of them, or possibly both of them, had changed their MO's, it was not likely that they would be very strong suspects. Yet, no matter how hard I tried, I couldn't see both of them being at the same place, at the same time, as being just a coincidence. If that were the case, there had to be some other reason for them to be in South Shore Park at the same time. A complete review of their criminal records was certainly in order.

I made a phone call to records and asked that Danny Minger's and Charley Mitken's arrest files be pulled so I could review them. While I was at it, I sent a list of the names of all the other potential witnesses to the records room clerk and requested that she check them out to see if any of them had records. If she found any others with criminal records, I wanted to see their arrest records as well. I needed to know if I was dealing with someone that I might not have heard of before or whose name I didn't immediately recognize.

It was going to take awhile for the clerk to check for arrest records and to pull those that were on the list. It was late and I was getting hungry. I had not eaten dinner yet. I checked out, left the office and went down to the police garage to get my car.

As I was entering the garage, I noticed someone standing in the shadows near the entrance to the police garage. There was no way of knowing who it might be, but it was pretty common for some of the officers to meet their wives or girlfriends in the police garage to pick up their dinners when they had to work the late shift.

As I approached my car, I kept an eye toward the shadow just to make sure it was not someone who might be there to do harm. I decided that it would be a good idea to get the person's attention and let him know that I had seen him. I was sure that if it had been someone waiting for one of the officers on duty to come down, they would not be so careful to hide themselves.

"You, come out in the open where I can see you," I called out as I stepped behind one of the police cars.

I waited for a moment, but when I didn't get a response I drew my 9mm automatic from under my coat. When I ask someone to show themselves and they don't, I tend to get a little nervous. I was not about to let a stranger get the drop on me if I could help it.

"You better come out, now," I said as I pointed my gun over the top of the car toward the shadow.

Slowly, a pair of hands began to show themselves from behind the large concrete pillar. They were followed by a tall, very skinny young man in his early twenties. As soon as he stepped out into the light, I could see that it was Danny Minger. He turned toward me and held his hands up so I could see that he was not carrying a weapon. It was easy to see that he was scared.

"Don't shoot, Detective McCord. I'm unarmed," he said, his voice showing how frightened he was.

"What are you doing in here, Danny?" I asked as I stepped out from behind the car.

"I was waiting for you."

"What do you want with me?"

"I saw you at South Shore Park this afternoon. I knew that if you were investigating that dead girl at the beach, you'd run across my name and come looking for me. I thought it would be better if I come to you first," he explained nervously as he glanced down at my gun.

"You can put your hands down, Danny," I said as I tucked my gun back under my coat.

Danny put his hands down and let out a sigh of relief. He was still a good twenty feet away from me. As he began walking toward me, a police officer came out of the building into the garage. Danny froze and looked toward the officer. His eyes were as big as saucers. For a second I thought that Danny was going to break and run, but he just stood there watching the officer walk to a police car, get in and drive away.

"What are you so nervous about, Danny?"

"You know I don't like this place. It gives me the willies. Is there a safe place where we can talk, someplace other than in the police station?"

"Sure. Have you had dinner?"

"Yes."

"Okay, you can join me for coffee," I suggested. "Come on."

"Where we going?"

"How about across the street to the cafe?"

"No, not there. That's where a lot of cops hang out. I don't want to go there. Not there."

"You would be safe there," I suggested.

"Not there," he insisted.

At first, I thought the reason that he didn't want to go to the cafe was because he was afraid of police officers in general, but my gut feeling told me that he had another reason for not wanting to be around so many policemen. There was something about the way his eyes looked at me, and the way he looked at the officer who had just walked through the garage. I got the feeling that there was more to it than his dislike for police officers. With as many times as he had been in a police station, I couldn't see him having this much fear of the place. He acted as if he was scared to death. But why, and of whom?

"What's the matter?"

"My life won't be worth a nickel if I'm seen talking to you, or any cop for that matter. Let's get out of here and go someplace else."

"Why, Danny?"

"I just don't want to be seen talking to you."

"Okay, over here."

I led him to my car and unlocked the door for him. As I went around to the other side to get in, he got in and quickly slid down in the seat so that it would be hard for anyone to see him. I got in and started the car. Once we were out on the street and had gone several blocks, he sat up.

"Okay, Danny. What's going on?"

"I want you to know that I had nothing to do with that girl's death."

"Okay. Let's say, at least for now, that I believe you. What do you know?"

I couldn't picture Danny coming to me unless he needed something. The way he was acting, I got the impression that he was looking for protection, but protection from whom? On the other hand, he wouldn't have taken the risk to come and find me unless he knew something, maybe something that could get him killed. I drove along as I waited for him to gather his thoughts as well as his courage.

"I was at the beach doing a little business when I saw Charley Mitken. I never saw him around South Shore Park before and I avoid him whenever possible. He hates me, you know. I was about to take off when one of the cops grabbed me and began questioning me. I didn't know what it was about until the cop told me about the dead girl, I swear."

"What kind of business were you doing in the park?" I asked as if I didn't already know.

"I was selling."

"Selling what?"

"You know, stuff."

I knew, all right. He was pushing drugs to some of the kids in the park.

"Who did you sell to, anyone I should know?"

"Yeah. Jonathan Ehman."

"Ehman?"

"Yeah, you know, the guy talking to that detective from the other precinct."

"Do you know Lieutenant Brooks?" I asked, suddenly very much interested in what Danny had to say.

"Yeah. So does Ehman."

Well, that answered one of my questions, but still didn't prove anything.

"When did you sell to Ehman?"

"About twenty or thirty minutes before he found the girl."

Now this was getting interesting. This simply confirmed that I needed to do an in-depth background check of Jonathan Ehman. I wanted to know everything there was to know about him, his friends and his enemies, who he knew and who knew him. It was beginning to look like my suspicions about Ehman had some merit and was becoming more than just a gut feeling.

"Tell me about Ehman. What kind of a mood was he in?"

"He was nervous as hell," Danny said. "He spent a lot of time looking out toward the lake, you know, as if he was expecting to see something out there. And he must have spent two hours walking up and down the beach."

"He was there that long?"

"Yeah. I saw him going up and down the beach at least an hour and a half before he spotted me and asked me for a fix."

"Have you sold to Ehman before?"

"Sure. I don't deal with strangers," Danny said.

"How long have you known him?"

"I don't know. Probably about a year or so, but I've never seen him so nervous. He was always cool, you know, sort of relaxed as if he had the whole world stuffed in his hip pocket. But not today."

"You have any idea as to why he was so nervous?"

"No."

"Do you usually sell to him in South Shore Park?"

"No. That was strange, too. I've never seen him on that side of town before, and I spend a lot of time at South Side Park. I usually run into him in the mall."

"What did you sell him?"

"A little pot. That's all he ever buys. I don't think he uses it much, but he was pretty nervous today."

I thought about that last statement as I pulled over to the curb in front of a small corner cafe that I had frequented when I was a patrolman. I looked over at Danny, still wondering how much of what he had told me I should believe.

"You said that you know Lieutenant Brooks. Did you see him in the park today?"

"Yeah. I saw him questioning Ehman in the park."

"Did you ever see the two of them together before today, or even earlier today in the park?"

"No," he said after giving it some thought.

Well, that took me nowhere. I was hoping that I could place Brooks and Ehman together in South Shore Park before the body was found. I was still having a hard time getting the idea out of my head that Brooks was involved in this whole thing in some way.

So far, Danny had provided me with some usable information, but nothing very exciting. I had learned a long time ago not to believe everything I'm told without checking it out. It was clear that Danny was trying to keep himself out of the middle, but the middle of what?

"I'm going in here to get something to eat. You want to join me? I'm buying."

Danny looked around, then shook his head indicating that he did not want to go inside. He opened the door and got out. He turned around and leaned on the roof of the car.

"Something I didn't tell you. I got a call from one of my regulars to meet someone at the park near the restrooms, close to the swings, at one o'clock sharp to make a sale. The girl never showed up."

"Who was it you were supposed to meet?"

"Just a girl, at least that's what I was told."

"What was her name?"

"They didn't tell me."

"What did she look like?"

"I don't know. Like I said, she never showed up. A friend said that she was okay and that I wasn't to worry about anything. She would know me and call me by name."

"I didn't think that you did business that way, not knowing who you are dealing with?"

"I usually don't, but she was recommended by one of my regular customers so I figured it would be okay."

"Who's your regular?"

"I can't tell you that. It wouldn't be good for business, or my health," he said with a grin.

I decided not to press him for more information right now. I could always have him picked up if I needed to pressure him for names. I felt it would be better that we part on a friendly note. I wanted him to believe that I didn't consider him a suspect to the murder even if I still considered him one. I was sure that he wouldn't run. For the time being, I wanted him out there where he might be able to find out more about what was going on.

"Okay. Danny, you know how to find me. If you learn anything that will help, let me know."

"Yes, sir."

"Danny, one more thing. Watch your back."

Danny nodded slightly, gave me just a hint of a smile, then turned and walked away. I watched until he turned the corner and disappeared.

I got out of the car and went into the cafe to sit down and enjoy the house specialty, a roast beef dinner. When I finished eating, I drove back to the precinct station and parked my car in the garage. All the way back, I thought about what Danny had said. There were still a lot of unanswered questions, but the one thing that kept running through my mind was why was Danny called to go to South Shore Park? Was it to make a sale to some girl? I had my doubts. Someone wanted him in the park at that time and place, but why?

When I got back to my desk, I found that there were six arrest files in my basket. Three I had counted on, Danny Minger's, Charley Mitken's and Jonathan Ehman's. It was the other three that caught my attention.

The first was that of Robert Goouchie, an old time muscle for some hood in Chicago. His criminal record indicated that he had been in prison until about three weeks ago. If my memory served me right, he had been in jail for a number of years, maybe fifteen or more. I had heard of him, but I hadn't had any personal contact with him.

The second was Joe Martonie. I had not remembered seeing his name on the lists of people in the park. It may have been spelled wrong or I just plan missed it. But this one I knew personally. It had been my pleasure to put him away about five years ago. I was sure that Martonie murdered an old man by running over him with a car after the old man reported several extortion attempts to the police. The jury didn't see it that way. They found Martonie guilty of involuntary manslaughter instead. He was sentenced to five years in the state prison, where he served less then three. If I remembered correctly, he had some connection to the Angelini family, possibly related to them somehow, I wasn't sure. His was one file I would need to spend a lot of time on.

The last arrest file was that of Travis Fox. This one was new to me. I didn't know anything about him, but a quick look through his file told me most of what I needed to know. This guy would not win any awards for nice guy of the year. Although his rap sheet was short, it read like Charley's. It appeared that Fox was as violent, brutal and mean a man as Charley.

I dropped the files down on my desk and leaned back in my chair. As I looked at the files, I was convinced that somewhere in all this paper was a clue to who had killed the girl. The only problem I had was to find the clue, then figure out who did it and why.

I had been up since early morning and I was too tired to make sense of anything at this late hour. I doubted that I would be able to see a clue if it jumped up off the desk and hit me on the nose. It was time to go home, get some rest and hit it again in the morning when I would be fresh. Maybe by that time, Jerry would be able to tell me at least who the victim was, and hopefully give me a little something to go on. Right now, I had nothing, except for a lot of guessing.

I reached across my desk and shut off the desk lamp. As I stood up, I pulled my coat off the back of the chair. I swung it over my shoulder and walked out of the office. When I got to the garage, I got in my car and drove home. I hadn't been in the door of my apartment for more then fifteen minutes before I was in bed and sound asleep.

CHAPTER THREE

Morning came a little too early to suit me. In fact, it came well before the sun was up. I had gone to sleep thinking about the names of those who had been in the park and found myself waking up thinking about them.

I lay in the darkness of my bedroom with my hands behind my head and my eyes closed as I tried to go back to sleep. It would be a couple of hours before my alarm would go off and a little more sleep would do me good.

The problem was that my mind was so cluttered with thoughts about my current case that I could not relax long enough to go back to sleep. There was no sense just lying there in bed and thinking, so I got up and fixed myself a cup of coffee.

Sitting down at the table with my coffee, I picked up a pen and began making a list of the names of those who I thought might even remotely have something to do with, or know something about the murder of the young woman. I didn't spend a lot of time thinking about the suspects, I just wrote down the names as they came into my head. When I finished writing, I looked down and read out loud each name that I had written. I guess I was hoping that by saying their names out loud one might pop out at me as the prime suspect.

I quickly noticed that I had included Lieutenant John Brooks among the names on my list. My first thought was that I had included his name simply because I didn't like him, or because I didn't trust him. I also thought that I might have included him because I had had a recent confrontation with him at South Shore Park, or because I still resented him for causing me to lose a case. It didn't seem right for me to include him on my list of suspects just because I didn't like him.

As I was about to scratch his name from the list, I hesitated. Why should I take his name off the list, I asked myself. He was in the park when the body was found, it appeared that he knew the person who claimed he had found the body, and I had gotten the impression that he didn't really want me to question Ehman, one of my suspects. I had less than that on some of the other ones that I considered suspects.

Although I had nothing concrete to go on, I felt that there was enough for me to leave his name on the list. I would leave it until there was something that would convince me that his name didn't belong there.

The more time I spent thinking about Brooks, the more I realized that I didn't know him very well. I did know that he came up through the ranks like the rest of us, but a little faster than most of us. That, in and of itself, was nothing to hold against him.

He seemed to be better dressed than the average detective on the force. He wore fairly expensive and well-tailored suits, not sport coats and slacks like most of us. He wore silk ties and shirts that can't be purchased at any J.C Penny's that I've ever been in. He also drove a much nicer and more expensive car than almost anyone else on the force. But then, a lot of people drove a nicer car than my beat up old Dodge. From what I had heard, he had a very exclusive apartment in one of the more affluent parts of town. But again, there was absolutely no evidence that would indicate that he had come by his money dishonestly.

All my speculation about Lieutenant Brooks proved nothing. There were a number of reasons why he could afford these things, other than being a cop on the take. His wife, if he has one, could have money. Good investments were another way to come by money honestly, or he could have inherited it. But my gut feelings still continued to tell me not to let go of him as a suspect until I was completely satisfied that he was not involved. I always try to go with my gut feelings, it's been right far more times than it's been wrong.

Almost unconsciously, I had underlined his name several times as I thought about him instead of scratching it off my list. I didn't like the idea of doing an investigation of a fellow police officer without at least something solid to go on, but in his case I'd make an exception. There were just too many little things that kept haunting me. Too many unanswered questions about him, and I wanted answers.

I leaned back in the chair and sipped my coffee. It was easy to see that this investigation was going to take a lot of time. It would take time to go through files and time to interview all the suspects. Time was what it was going to take to find out who killed the girl and dumped her body on the lakefront. And it was beginning to look like it was going to take time to find out who she was.

I was certain that among my list of suspects was the person or persons who would lead me to the killer. It was entirely possible that one or more of them on the list was the killer, or was directly involved in the girl's death in some way.

I drank down the last of my coffee then went into the bathroom to take a shower. The warm water flowing over me cleared my head and allowed me to think a little clearer. When I finished showering, I shaved, got ready for work and drove to the police station. All the time I was going over and over my list of suspects in my head.

I arrived at my desk just shortly before eight. After getting another cup of coffee, I sat down and looked at the pile of arrest records that had been left there from last night. I took a deep breath and pulled the first file off the pile and opened it.

It was the arrest record of Robert Goouchie. The first thing I noticed was that Goouchie had to be in his late sixties, or early seventies. In looking over the records of his arrests, I quickly discovered that he had spent over half his life behind bars with the last of several long stretches being for second-degree murder. The notes indicated that he had agreed to a plea bargain down from first-degree murder to second-degree murder in exchange for blowing the whistle on some big Chicago mob leader. Goouchie got off with only fifteen years, but the Chicago hood was sentenced to a very long time. A note in the file indicated that the Chicago mob leader died some years ago while still in prison.

The deeper I got into Goouchie's arrest record, the less I felt that he was a very likely suspect. He had gotten out of prison only a few months ago. He was not from the area, and I felt that he was just a little too old to change his ways and become a hit man. Although Chicago is not that far from Milwaukee, there was no indication in the file that he really knew anyone here. I wondered if he had come to Milwaukee to simply live out his life in peace, or if he had some other reason for being here.

I set Goouchie's arrest record off to one side as I made a mental note to check up on him, just in case. If he was not involved in the murder, it might be a good idea to find out why he came here from prison.

I reached out and picked up the second file from the pile of arrest records. It was the arrest record of Joe Martonie. I carefully reviewed his file, although I already knew him. It didn't take long for me to refresh my memory of this man, and to get a good picture of the type of man I would be dealing with here.

Martonie had been arrested on numerous charges of assault, including assaulting an officer, threatening people with a gun, and other charges that were minor when compared to his list of assault arrests. He had all the makings of a mob muscle, the type that would break your legs for not paying your debt to his boss on time, but this was not news to me.

I also noted that he was married to one of Frank Angelini's younger sisters, Marie. That sure made it clear that he was a member of the Angelini family. There was no doubt in my mind that a man with his talents would be considered a welcome asset to the family organization. Although he was muscle for the family, I doubted that he would be the one that did the killing. After all, he was a little too close to the top man. The Angelini family couldn't afford to have a murder investigation that close to the top man, namely Frank Angelini. Joe Martonie was going to be hard to get to for questioning. The Angelini family was very tight and very protective of their people.

Just as I was about to pick up another file, the phone rang. I reached across the stack of files and picked up the phone.

"Detective McCord, may I help you?"

"Nick, this is Jerry in pathology. I think I have something that might interest you."

"What is it?"

"If you've got a minute, I'd like you to come down to the lab."

"All right, I'll be there in a few minutes," I replied and hung up the phone.

I wondered what it was Jerry had found that was so interesting he needed to see me in person. I pushed back my chair and stood up. As I was reaching for my coat on the back of my chair, I noticed Captain Sinclair coming out of his office and walking toward me.

"Nick, how's it going?"

"Morning, Captain. You look like you have something on your mind?" I asked, ignoring his question.

"I do. I got a call this morning from the captain at West Park Division."

"Oh, really?"

"Yes. It seems he's not very happy with the lack of respect you showed Lieutenant Brooks yesterday."

"Really? Well, that might be because I don't have any respect for Lieutenant Brooks," I replied kind of enjoying the fact that I had made the lieutenant a little unhappy. "I must have touched a nerve."

"You sure as hell did. He wants an immediate apology from you, in writing. What do you say?"

"I say you can tell him not to hold his breath. I wouldn't be surprised if Lieutenant Brooks was involved in the case I'm working on up to the neck of his hundred dollar silk shirt."

"Can you prove that?"

"No, not yet."

"What makes you think that he's involved?"

"Gut feeling, mostly."

"Well, you better have more than gut feelings before you spread that around."

"I don't want it spread around at all. I've worked with you for years. We know each other pretty well. You know that I don't go around making accusations without some kind of proof. If I find that Lieutenant Brooks is not involved, I'll go over to West Park Division and apologize to the lieutenant, and to the captain, in person."

"I'll hold you to that, but until then I'll expect you to stay away from Lieutenant Brooks."

"What if I have to question him?"

"If that should become necessary, I will handle it, all of it."

There was no doubt about what the captain meant. I would have to have some pretty solid proof that Brooks was involved before he would be brought in for questioning. It was also clear that I would not be allowed to make the arrest or question him without Captain Sinclair present.

"I understand," I said, knowing that it had to be that way.

"Where are you headed now?"

"I got a call from Jerry Kowalski in Pathology. He said he had something that he wanted me to see. He's working on the autopsy of that girl found on the beach."

"Well, you better get down there. Nick, keep me posted. If we have a bad cop on the force, I don't want him around any more than you do."

Joe was a good man and a good cop. I gave him a slight nod and left the office. As I turned to go out the door, I glanced back toward my desk and saw Joe staring off toward the wall. I was sure that he was wondering if we had a bad cop in our midst, a thought that didn't set well with me, either.

When I arrived in the lab, Jerry met me with a big grin of self-satisfaction. Kind of like when someone knows something you don't, but can hardly wait to see your reaction when you're told. He motioned me to follow him into an autopsy room. Laid out on a stainless steel table, only partially covered with a sheet, was the body of the young girl who had been found on the beach. I found it difficult to take my eyes off her as she looked so young, and so dead.

"Nick," Jerry said to get my attention.

"Yeah," I said as I turned and looked at him.

"I've completed the autopsy and found some very interesting things."

"Like what?"

"First of all, the cause of death was not the .25 caliber bullet hole we found in the back of her head."

"It wasn't?"

"No. I think the cause of death was an overdose of cocaine. I'll know for sure when I get all the lab studies done."

"What? You mean that someone shot her after she was already dead?" I asked, almost not believing what he had told me.

"Right. She was dead before she was shot, that much I'm sure of."

"That doesn't make sense."

"I have something else that doesn't make sense. I found only one injection site on her entire body."

"Just one?"

"Yes, one. I don't think this girl was a user."

"Maybe, it was her first time to use a needle?"

"No. I mean, I don't believe that she had ever used the stuff before. There are no other needle marks, there is no damaged tissue in her nose from sniffing the stuff, there is no indication at all that she has ever used cocaine or any other drug, expect for birth control pills."

"Maybe, it was her first time and she couldn't handle the stuff?" I asked.

"That's a possibility, but I don't think so. I think someone held her down and injected her with a lethal dose of almost pure cocaine. Remember the marks on her face? Those marks, along with the other marks I found on her body indicate that she had struggled with someone shortly before she died. There are bruises on her upper arms, wrists, shoulders and legs that are consistent with what one could expect to see if the victim struggled while being held down."

"Was she raped?"

"No. There was no indication that she had been sexually assaulted. My bet is that the blood tests will show a very high concentration of cocaine in her blood, more than anyone would even consider using."

"Why would someone shoot her up with enough cocaine to kill her then shoot her in the head? It doesn't make any sense."

"Sorry, Nick, but that's your department. You're the detective. It's your job to make sense of things like that. It's my job to tell you what caused the victim to die."

"Yeah," I replied as I thought about what Jerry had told me.

"One more thing, I found this pinned on the collar of her blouse," he said as he held out a small delicately fashioned gold broach.

I took the broach from his hand and examined it very carefully. I'm no expert, but it reminded me of some of the jewelry that I had seen on another case I had worked on not too long ago. Although I don't know much about old jewelry, I know someone who does. She would be able to tell me everything there is to know about the broach.

"Can I borrow this broach for a few days?"

"Sure, as long as you sign for it."

"Any prints on it?"

"Only hers. I didn't find it until I took her blouse off. It was hidden inside her blouse, probably from the struggle."

"You have any other surprises for me?" I asked as I signed the evidence release form for the broach.

"No, I don't think so. I might have more for you after I finish with the lab tests."

"Do you know how much time she spent in the water?"

"Not for sure, but I don't think she was in the lake very long. If I had to guess, I would say the body was dumped on the beach at the edge of the water. I'm sure that she was not dumped out in the lake and her body washed up later."

"What makes you say that?"

"Her clothes were not completely saturated with lake water which would indicate she hadn't been completely submerged in the lake. Also, there wasn't the usual residue from the oil scum and other pollutants that are normally found in the lake and that we see embedded in the clothing of those who are pulled out of the lake after several hours in the water."

"Are you sure?"

"Well, not a hundred percent, but I don't think she was dumped in the lake. Also, there's the fact that her skin was not mottled like that of someone who had been in the water for a long time which means she was found shortly after she was put in the water. My best guess would be probably within, say, an hour at the most."

"Anything else?"

"Not at the moment. I'll let you know if anything else turns up. I hope that helps."

"It does. Thanks again," I said as I turned and walk out of the lab.

Nothing is ever easy, I thought as I tried to put the pieces of the puzzle together. Why would someone kill this girl in the first place? But the question I found more interesting was why would someone go to the trouble of killing a person with cocaine, then shoot that person in the back of the head to make it look like a hit killing? Was it supposed to look like a hit killing to direct suspicion away from someone or toward someone?

As I rode up the elevator to my office, I examined the broach in my hand. The workmanship of the broach was unique. There was a delicately carved profile of a woman in what looked to me to be ivory. The border around the ivory appeared to be white gold and was most likely hand tooled. Rolling the broach over in my hand, I noticed that the broach and catch looked as if they had been handmade. It seemed to me to be somewhat unusual. But, as I said before, I'm not an expert on jewelry, and right now I needed an expert.

This old piece of jewelry brought back some very pleasant memories of a woman whom I would love to see again. A woman who could most likely tell me the history of the broach, right down to how old it was, where it was originally made, and maybe, even who made it. And if I was really lucky, she might even be able to tell me who it was made for.

I sat down at my desk and let my thoughts of Doctor Monica Barnhart fill my head. It had been a long time since I had talked to her and even longer since I had seen her. It seemed that we both had gotten so wrapped up in our jobs that we had lost contact with each other. I wondered if she would remember me with the same sort of pleasant memories I had of her.

"Nick!"

Damn! I didn't want my thoughts interrupted right now. I was really getting to enjoy them. I looked up and found Joe standing in front of my desk starring down at me.

"Nick, you okay?"

"Yeah. I was just thinking."

"About what?"

"Oh, nothing important," I said not wanting to explain anything just now. "What is it?"

"I got a call from the front desk. It seems a lady called and wanted to report a missing girl. The description the woman gave the desk sergeant sounds a lot like the girl found on the beach. I think you should get over there and see what you can find out. Maybe, you can get a picture of the missing girl," he said as he handed me a piece of paper with an address on it.

"I'll get right on it," I said as I stood up and grabbed my coat.

I took the elevator to the police garage and signed out a car. Within minutes, I was on my way across town to the address Joe had given me.

The late morning traffic was slow, but it gave me time to think. The name of the missing girl was Robin Flower. I remembered what Danny had told me last night about the girl that he was to meet in the park. I wondered if she was the girl Danny was to have met. I also wondered if the girl in the morgue could be Robin Flower.

CHAPTER FOUR

It took me a little while to find the address that Captain Sinclair had given me. It was in one of the older parts of the city where the houses were close together and the streets were narrow. Most of the houses were rundown and in need of repair. A large number of people with low incomes lived in the neighborhood. It was also well known for its drugs, booze and gang activities.

The good honest people who lived in the area were afraid of everyone, especially strangers. They were afraid to talk to the police for fear that one of the gangs in the area might fire bomb their home, or beat them or a family member to death. As a result, the gangs were relatively free to roam the streets and terrorize anyone they came in contact with. Police cars patrolled the streets day and night, but without help from the local residents to point out the criminals there was little that the police could do to put a stop to it.

As I pulled up to the curb and stopped the car, I got the feeling that behind every dingy curtain, in every rundown house, there were eyes watching every move I made. It was not the type of neighborhood I wanted to be in alone, but I had a job to do.

I looked up at the house. It didn't look like the type of a house that the young girl I had seen lying on the beach and in the morgue would have come from. She had been wearing some very nice and expensive clothes. They were the kind of clothes that would not normally be found in the closets of houses like these. The brooch she had been wearing was very uptown, expensive and I would guess rather rare. But on the other hand, she would not have been the first pretty girl to find her way out of a neighborhood like this and move up to a better part of town. I had to ask myself if the price she paid was worth it. I didn't think so, and I was sure she wouldn't either if she had known what the price was going to be.

As I got out of my car, I noticed several young men sitting on the porch of the house across the street. They wore the colored headbands of one of the better-known local gangs. They never took their eyes off me as I walked around the car and up the sidewalk to the front door. I knocked on the door, then glanced back across the street to see if the gang members were still on the porch. A couple of them stood up and leaned against the railing. They stared at me as if trying to intimidate me, but that was all. I was sure that they knew I was a cop.

My attention was brought back to the house as I could hear someone moving around inside. A curtain in a window near the door opened slightly and a woman peered out at me. It was clear from the expression on her face that she was curious as to who I was and what I wanted.

"I'm Detective McCord of the police department," I said as I held out my badge and ID card for her to see. "I understand that you reported a missing girl. Is that correct?"

I watched as the woman moved away and the curtain fell back over the window. There was the distinct sound of several locks being turned before the door opened. The woman studied my badge for a few seconds from behind the screen door then looked up at me.

"Come in, please," she said as she unlocked the screen door and stepped back.

I opened the door and walked into the house. She led me into the living room. Although the house appeared to be rundown on the outside, it was very neat and clean, and quite pleasant inside.

"I'm Rose Flower. Please, sit down," she said politely.

Rose appeared to be in her early to mid forties and was a nice looking woman. Her facial features were similar to those of the dead girl. I assumed that she was the dead girl's mother, but I had to be sure.

"Thank you."

"Would you care for a cup of coffee?"

"No, thank you," I replied as I sat down on the sofa.

"I suppose you want to get started?"

"Yes, if you don't mind. I understand that you reported your daughter missing, is that correct?"

"Yes."

"What's your daughter's name?"

"Robin Flower."

"Do you happen to have a picture of her?"

"Yes," she replied, then stood up.

She walked over to an old piano and picked up a high school graduation picture. Rose handed me the picture.

The girl in the picture was the same girl that we had in the morgue, but there was a great deal of difference between the two. The one in the picture was not only beautiful, but she looked happy and very much alive.

"She's very pretty. When did you see her last?"

"About a week ago. She always comes to see me on Wednesday. This past Wednesday, she didn't come," Rose said with a worried look on her face.

"She always came to see you on Wednesday?"

"Every Wednesday without fail. That is until this past Wednesday."

"Do you know who any of her friends might be?"

"I don't know any of her friends anymore. She moved out a little over a year ago and made new friends. I guess I can't blame her for wanting to get out to here," she said as she looked around the room.

"Do you know where she lives now?"

"No, not really. She talks about her fancy apartment on the west side of town, but I don't know where it is. I wish I did, but I have been stubborn and wouldn't go see it," she explained as tears came to her eyes. "She has been after me to move in with her, but I refused. I told her I didn't belong in no fancy uptown apartment."

I got this strange feeling that she already knew her little girl was dead. It was not that she had been told, but rather a mother's instinct, I suppose. I certainly didn't want to be the one to tell her, but I didn't see that I had much choice.

"Did she, or does she have a boyfriend?"

"Yes. I met him just once. He seemed nice enough, but I could tell he didn't like being in this house."

"What makes you say that?"

"I think he is pretty wealthy and didn't want to be seen in this neighborhood. I think it made him uncomfortable."

"Do you know his name?"

"Tony, Tony Angelini, I believe. It was something like that, something Italian sounding. As I said, I only met him once."

If my memory served me right, Tony Angelini was the only son of Frank Angelini. If I was right about Lieutenant Brooks's connection with the Angelini family, this might just help explain why Brooks was at the park when the body was found. The Angelini family didn't need to have a bunch of cops nosing around in their business. If Lieutenant Brooks was on their payroll, it would be his job to see to it that any investigation into the death of Robin Flower would lead away from the Angelini family. But I had no proof that Brooks was on Angelini's payroll.

"I'm sorry to have to tell you this, Mrs. Flower, but I believe your daughter died yesterday."

She just sat there and stared at me. The color went from her face and she turned white as a ghost. I thought for a minute that she was going to faint. Suddenly, she took in a deep breath and tears began to fill her eyes and roll down her cheeks.

"Are you sure?" she asked, her voice choking on the words.

"A girl fitting the description of your daughter was found on the beach at South Shore Park yesterday."

"Oh, God no," she said in a deep, hushed whisper.

"How did it happen?" she asked between sobs.

"We don't know yet. It's still under investigation, but we believe she was murdered."

Rose just looked at me as if she was in shock, which I'm sure she was. She didn't say anything as she sat in the chair with tears running down her face.

I never really knew how to handle situations like this, and always felt so helpless when I was called on to notify the next of kin of the death of a family member. I sat there and watched her as she covered her face with her hands and cried openly. There was nothing that I could do except wait for her to regain some control of herself.

When her crying subsided a little, I asked, "Is there anything I can do?"

"Where is she, where's my baby?"

"She's in the morgue downtown. I can make arrangements for you to see her, if you like."

"Yes, please."

"Do you have transportation?"

"No. My car was stolen last week."

"I'll make arrangements for someone to pick you up. They will call you this afternoon to arrange everything," I said as I stood up. "I can find my way out."

As I walked over to the door, I glanced back to see her still sitting in the chair, her chin in her hands and tears flowing down her face as she sobbed. I hated to leave her like that, but there was nothing more I could do.

I got in my car and drove back downtown. As soon as I arrived at the office, I made the arrangements for a car to pick up Mrs. Flower and bring her to the morgue so she could identify her daughter.

As I sat at my desk to think over all the information I had so far, my first thought was that I needed to find out where Robin Flower lived. I immediately contacted the Records Department and requested they do all they could to find Miss Flower's address.

I decided that it was also time to talk to Danny again. One of the things I wanted to know was the name of his "special customer", the one who told him to sell drugs to the girl. I had a feeling who it was, but I needed to hear it from him.

I made a quick call and had an APB put out on Danny Minger. I wanted him picked up and taken into custody for questioning. After that, it was time to wait. While I was waiting, I reviewed several of the files on my desk.

* * * *

It was getting late. I had spent the entire afternoon going over the arrest records stacked on my desk. At this point, I still had nothing solid to go on. So far I had been unable to eliminate any of my suspects.

The Records Department had not been able to come up with an address for Robin's apartment, but I did get a call telling me that Danny Minger had been found and picked up. I directed the desk sergeant to have Danny delivered to me, immediately. It took only a few minutes for the officer who had picked him up to bring him to the office.

"Good evening, Danny," I said as he was gently, but firmly, pushed into a chair along side my desk by the arresting officer.

"I got nothing to say to you," he said defiantly.

"You can take the cuffs off him. He's not going anywhere," I said to the arresting officer while ignoring Danny's outburst.

I waited and watched Danny as the officer removed the cuffs from him. He was putting on a good front, but I knew that at the first sign that he might have to sit in a jail cell Danny would start talking.

"I told you everything I know, so you might as well let me go," he announced after the officer removed the cuffs.

"You haven't told me quite everything. In fact, you haven't told me anything," I replied, then waited for the officer to leave.

"I want the name of your special customer," I said as I watched his face turn a little pale. "Remember, the name you wouldn't tell me yesterday."

"I'm not going to tell you today, either," he said, but the tone of his voice was beginning to show just how frightened he was becoming.

"Danny, you don't seem to understand the situation here," I said softly with a slight grin on my face. "You don't have a choice. You WILL tell me his name, and you WILL tell me, now."

"I can't, my life won't be worth a nickel," he pleaded.

"Hell, Danny, look around. Your life isn't worth a nickel now," I said growing a little impatient with him. "Every police officer on duty across the city knows that I put an APB out on you. You should be glad that I got to you instead of Lieutenant Brooks."

I didn't have any idea what kind of a response I would get from Danny by throwing out Brooks's name, but it was worth a try. When I saw his reaction, I don't know who was more surprised. Danny's eyes got big and his face flushed. There was no doubt in my mind that Danny was scared to death of Brooks, but why? What did he know about Brooks?

"Okay, Danny, let's have it. Who is your special customer?"

"You've got to protect me."

The fear for his life was clear in his voice.

"I'll find a safe place for you, but you have to tell me what I want to know."

Danny looked down at the floor as he contemplated his options, which I'm sure he realized were few to none. He knew that at this point it didn't matter if he told me or not.

He had been picked up and questioned. Anyone who knew Danny would figure that he would break and talk.

"Okay. It's Fox, Travis Fox. Now you have to find a safe place for me to hide," he demanded. "You promised."

I had to admit that I was the one surprised. Although I didn't want to believe it, I had convinced myself that it had been Brooks. I didn't know much about Fox. I needed to find out more about the guy, and further study of his rap sheet would be the best place to start.

"Tell me what you know about him?"

"I don't know much about him. He used to buy drugs from me awhile back, then I didn't hear from him for a long time. Suddenly I get this call from him, at least it sounded like him, telling me to sell drugs to the girl I told you about yesterday."

"What do you mean it sounded like him?"

"It sounded like him."

"Then you're not sure it was him?"

"Not a hundred percent sure. No."

I never knew just how much of what Danny told me was the truth. I had to think about what he said and look into this Fox character.

"Well, what about me?" Danny asked interrupting my thoughts.

"I've got just the place for you."

"Where?"

"In a quiet little room in the basement. It has padded walls and floor, and is out of the reach of anyone who might get himself arrested just to do you in."

"In the nut cell?" he yelled angrily. "No way."

"Think, Stupid. Can you think of a safer place until we can get this all sorted out?" I said in a whisper hoping that he would calm down before he announced to the whole world where I was going to hide him.

I could see that he was turning over what I had said in his head. If he was on the street, he was a dead man and he knew it.

"No. I guess not," he finally conceded.

"Good. I'll take you down myself."

I took my cuffs from my belt and cuffed Danny before leaving the office. The last thing I wanted was for him to get away from me. I would never be able to protect him in the outside world.

Escorting him to the elevator, we rode down to the basement where the jail was located. The head jailer was a personal friend of mine. After briefly explaining the situation to him, he took Danny and locked him up in a private, padded cell away from the other inmates. As soon as I was sure that Danny was safely hidden away, I returned to my office.

I sat down at my desk and picked up the file on Travis Fox. I reviewed his arrest record, including the arresting officers, the officers that handled the investigations, and the findings as a result of those investigations. In the course of close examination of the reports, I discovered one very interesting piece of information that I had not really expected to find. It seemed that every time Travis Fox had been arrested and then released due to insufficient evidence, Lieutenant Brooks had been one of, if not the only, investigating officer.

This was one bit of information that I planned to keep to myself for a little while. Although it gave the appearance of Lieutenant Brooks being a cop on the take, in and of itself, it was not enough evidence to take to Captain Sinclair. It certainly did not connect Brooks to the death of Robin Flower, at least not yet.

I also discovered in the file that Travis Fox worked in a jewelry store. I found it a little hard to believe that an enforcer for the mob would be working in a jewelry store. His arrest record was more like what I would have expected to find of a person who worked in a junkyard. After all, his police records indicated that he was mean enough to be a junkyard dog.

Yet, closer examination of his file indicated that he had worked in his father's jewelry store when he was a kid before his father died, and now worked with his uncle. A look at his police photo showed that he was a rather handsome man who would probably appeal to the ladies. If his demeanor was half as pleasant as he appeared in the photo, then why not? He certainly would not be the first person to live two completely different lives.

Another interesting piece of information that I found in his file was that he had not been arrested in the past eighteen months, or so, for anything. That did not seem to fit with the pattern of the previous five or six years. Prior to the eighteen months, he had been arrested at least two or three times a year for something.

It was starting to get late and I was getting tired. It was time to put things up for the night, besides I had a phone call to make. I took my coat from the back of the chair, checked out and drove home.

As soon as I got in my apartment, I sat down and picked up the phone. I wondered what kind of reaction I would get from Monica since I had not called her for some time. The phone rang only three times before it was answered.

"Hello?"

I would know that sexy voice anywhere. Just the sound of her voice made me want to sit quietly and listen to her, but I thought I'd better say something before she hung up on me.

"Hi. This is Nick."

"Oh, Nick. It's been so long," she said excitedly.

"I know, and I'm sorry about that. I've been wanting to call, but never seemed to find the time."

"That's a pretty lame excuse, Nicolas McCord," she reminded me.

"I know, but then I haven't heard from you, either."

"That's true," she conceded.

"It's good to hear your voice again."

"Yours, too. I've been thinking about you a lot lately. I was thinking I should call you to see if you might like to get together for a weekend sometime soon," she said hopefully.

"I would love that, I really would. But I'm afraid my reason for calling isn't so romantic. I have an ulterior motive for calling you."

"Oh, really?"

"I need your expertise," I said almost apologetically.

"What's going on?" she asked, her voice taking on a serious tone.

"I'm working on a murder case," I said.

"Is it that one I heard on the news, the one where the young woman was found dead on the beach?"

"Yes, I'm afraid so."

"How can I help?"

"A brooch was found on the victim's clothing. It looks to me like it might be a very old brooch and of some value. I would like you to take a look at it and tell me what you can about it."

"Nick, I'd be happy to. Will it help your case?" she asked.

"I don't know, but it might."

"When would you like me to come?"

"As soon as you can?" I asked, hoping that she would be able to come in the next few days.

"I can be there tomorrow afternoon. Will that be all right?"

I hadn't figured on her dropping everything to come immediately, but I must admit seeing her again would certainly make my day.

"Sure. Will you be driving in?"

"I'll fly in if you'll pick me up at the airport. My car is temporarily out of service. They're waiting for a part to fix it."

"Certainly. That would be great."

"Nick, should I get a motel room?" she asked softly.

"You can if you want, but you are always welcome to stay with me at my place, if you like."

"I like, I like very much," she said excitedly in that soft sexy voice that was always a pleasure to hear. "Will we be able to spend some time together?"

"I'm sure we can find some time. In fact, I'll make time."

We talked for just a few minutes more before we hung up. After hanging up the phone, I couldn't help but think about her. Here was a woman, Monica Barnhart, who was a professor of history at the University of Wisconsin and an expert in her field, yet one of the sexiest women I've ever had the pleasure of knowing.

It was easy for me to picture her in my mind, her long blond hair and cobalt blue eyes, the smooth flowing lines of her fantastic figure and the gentle sway of her hips as she walked. I had to smile to myself when I thought about how excited she made me feel by just hearing her voice. It even made me feel a little guilty because I hadn't called her sooner. I had waited until I needed her expertise before calling her.

Needless to say, I went to bed feeling very happy that she wanted to come and visit for a while. No matter how short our time together might be, I knew that it would be a time that we would remember.

CHAPTER FIVE

I woke early to the sounds of birds singing in the tree just outside my apartment window. It was kind of strange, but I hadn't really noticed them before. I guess I was just too busy with other things to have noticed. However, on this morning I had a very special woman on my mind. It always made me smile just to think of her.

The reason I got up so early was that I didn't want Monica to see my apartment in such a mess. I spent the first couple of hours of my day cleaning, straightening up the place and changing the bedding. Once I was satisfied that it was presentable, I drove to the police station. I had a lot of work to do before I could even think about spending any free time with Monica.

As I walked into the station, I observed an elderly gentleman sitting on one of the benches. I didn't pay a whole lot of attention to him, as it was normal to have people sitting around waiting to see one of the officers about one thing or another.

"McCord," the desk sergeant called out as I walked past the front desk.

"Yeah," I replied as I turned and stepped up to the desk.

"There's someone here to see you," he said as he glanced over at the old man.

I looked from the sergeant to the old man, but I didn't recognize him. I looked back at the sergeant. I must have had a big question mark stamped on my forehead when I looked back at him.

"He said that if you weren't looking for him now, you soon would be. He says his name is Robert Goouchie, or something like that."

I turned back and looked at him again. So this was Goouchie, the tough mob enforcer for a big time Chicago hood. He didn't look much like an enforcer, now. The years he had served in prison must have been hard on him. He looked like a tired old man that had been around for a very long time. If I had to guess, I would have guessed that he was much older then the late sixties I knew him to be.

"Give me a minute then send him back to my desk."

The sergeant nodded and I walked back to my desk. I hung my coat over the back of the chair and sat down. I pulled Goouchie's file from the stack of files on the desk and quickly glanced through it. His arrest file was thick, but contained nothing about any arrests here in Milwaukee. Everything in his file was from Chicago.

I looked up and saw Mr. Goouchie walking toward me. He walked rather slowly and was slightly stooped over. He looked frail and weak, not what I would have expected of a mob enforcer. I guess I even felt a little sorry for him.

"Detective McCord, I'm Bob - - -, Robert Goouchie. I suspect that - - you want to talk - - to me."

"Sit down, Mr. Goouchie," I said as I pointed to a chair next to my desk.

He pulled up a chair and sat down. He did not appear to be in very good health and I wondered what it was that he wanted.

"I figured that - - you would be wanting - - to talk to me about - - what I was doing in - - the park where that - - young girl was found dead."

He stopped to take a few short, labored breaths. From the way he talked and looked, it led me to believe that he suffered from severe emphysema, or some other type of lung disease that made it difficult for him to breath.

"You're right about that, but I would have come to your place. You didn't have to come here."

"Well, you see - - my landlady doesn't know - - I'm an ex-con. I would like - - it to stay that - - way. I don't need cops - - coming to see me."

"I understand."

I watched him as he took another moment to catch his breath. Gradually, I became less and less interested in him as a suspect. I doubted that he would have had the strength to force Robin to take a shot of cocaine, or to carry her any distance. However, I was interested in anything that he might have seen while he was in the park that would help me find the girl's killer.

"Tell me, Mr. Goouchie, we know you were in the park when the body was found. Did you see anything, anything that might help me find out who did it?"

"There were two - - men in the park - - that day - - that I know. I don't know - - them personally - - ,but I know - - who they are - - by reputation.

"Joe Martonie - - was one. He is a - - muscle for the - - Angelini family. But I'm sure - - you know that.

"The other was - - Travis Fox. He's from - - Chicago. I heard about him - - while in the - - joint. He came up - - here when my - - old boss died. I don't know who - - he is mixed up - -with, but the Angelini - - family would be my - - guess. Don't turn - - your back on him. He's dangerous."

Everything that I had been able to find out up to this point seemed to be pointing to the Angelini family as being involved in the death of the young girl. But there was something very wrong with the picture that was forming in my head. There appeared to be just too many people who had some kind of a connection to the Angelini family in the park that day. It was almost as if the Angelini family was having a picnic in the park. I doubted very much that the Angelini family would have a picnic in such a public place. They were a very close knit and very private family. It just didn't make any sense.

"Fox is originally from Milwaukee," I said.

"Maybe, but he - - spent a lot of time - - in Chicago."

"Did you see anyone around the part of the beach where the body was found before the young man pulled the girl up on the beach? Maybe, a car or a boat just off shore?"

"No."

"Did you see anything that seemed strange, or unusual?"

"I did see one - - thing that might be - - of interest to you."

"And what was that?"

"There was a - - dark blue unmarked - - police car parked in - - the parking lot with - - an officer inside. It was parked there - - for at least a - - couple of hours before - - the body was found."

Now this was something that stirred my interest. Lieutenant Brooks had driven off in a dark blue unmarked police car when Captain Sinclair had sent him packing.

"How do you know it was a police car?"

"I've seen enough - - of them. The officer was a - - tall, very well - - dressed man. He was wearing - - a medium gray suit - - and carried an automatic - - under his left arm - - in a shoulder holster."

It was clear that this old man knew what he saw, and that he paid attention to detail. It was no wonder that he had lived as long as he had. He knew what to look for and how to survive.

"Could you identify the man in the police car?" I asked, knowing from his description that it was most likely Lieutenant Brooks.

"Yes, but - - I won't."

"Why not?"

"I have a sister - - that lives here. I moved - - here to be close - - to what's left of - - my family before - - I die. I don't need - - any more trouble. I've had enough - - over the years. I just want - - to live out - - what's left of - - my life in peace."

"Then why did you come in and tell me all this?"

"To keep you - - from coming and - - banging on my door. I like it - - where I am and - - I don't want - - to have to move.

"I've told you - - all that I - - know. Now I hope - - you will leave - - me alone."

Here was the link that might tie Lieutenant Brooks in with the killing of Robin Flower and I was about to let him walk out the door without pressing him for more information. I felt sorry for the old man. It was clear that he had little life left. He had paid his debt to society and had every right to be left alone.

"Mr. Goouchie, here is my card. If you think of anything else that might be of help, I would appreciate it if you would give me a call. I will not promise you that I won't come to see you, but if I have to, I'll be as discreet as possible."

As he stood up, he looked at me as if he was trying to decide if I meant what I had said. Slowly, a slight grin came over his face. He nodded slightly, then turned and walked away. I watched him until he turned down the hall and disappeared from sight.

This man had been through a lot in his lifetime. The amazing thing was that he was one of the few old time mob enforcers for a crime boss who had lived to tell about it. Most of them didn't last long, especially if they were involved in territorial disputes. They usually ended up dead, especially if they were thinking of retiring. Their bosses didn't want them running around loose with all they knew.

My thoughts were suddenly interrupted when the phone on my desk began to ring. I reached over and picked up the receiver.

"McCord, may I help you?"

"Nick, this is Jerry. You got a minute?"

"Sure, what is it?"

"I thought you would like to know that I found pieces of colored confetti in the girl's hair."

"Confetti? Where would she get confetti in her hair?"

"Hey, I'm not the detective, you are," Jerry reminded me again. "Based on what was in her stomach, I'd say she had been to a party within, oh, three or four hours at the most before she died.

"Oh, one more thing. The girl was dead before she was put in the water, and she was most likely put in the lake right where she was found. I didn't find any beach sand in her clothes except for where she was dragged up on the beach. If she had washed up in the beach, I would expect to find beach sand all over her clothes."

"Thanks," I said as I hung up the phone.

I leaned back in the chair and thought about what I had to go on so far. It was time to find her boyfriend, Tony Angelini, and have a talk with him. I wasn't sure where he lived, but I knew it wouldn't be hard to find him.

I reached over and picked up the phone. I placed a call to records and asked them to pull up on their computer the last known address of Tony Angelini. It took them about two minutes to get me his address. I also asked them if they had found an address for Robin Flower. They said that they had found it. I half expected her address to be the same as the one for Tony Angelini, but to my surprise it turned out to be a different address. If I had known that she did not live with Tony, I would have pressed records to find it.

I figured that I had just made a very big mistake in my investigation by not pressing the records department for Robin's address. Every minute that I delayed in getting to her apartment and going over it, gave her killer or killers more time to get rid of any evidence that might be there. I immediately placed a call to Captain Sinclair.

"Captain, this is Nick."

"What's up?"

"I want authorization to have a patrol car go to Robin Flower's apartment in the Kilbourn Park District and seal the apartment until I can get there. I don't want them to let anyone, and I mean anyone, in her apartment until after I've had a chance to search it."

"I take it you're referring to Lieutenant Brooks?"

"Yes. It may be too late already."

"Okay, go for it."

As soon as I hung up, I called the communication center and had a patrol car dispatched with orders to let no one under any circumstances into Robin Flower's apartment without clearing it through me first. It took about ten minutes to get a call back from communications center informing me that a car was at Robin's apartment and they had the apartment sealed off.

A quick check of my watch told me that I had just enough time to drive to Robin's apartment and take a quick look around before I had to be at the airport to pick up Monica. I grabbed my jacket and headed out the door.

It took me about thirty minutes to get from the police garage to Robin's apartment. I pulled up to the curb and stopped. I glanced around as I got out of my car. A dark blue sedan was parked down the block near the corner. It was impossible to tell who was in the car because of glare on the windshield, but I could see someone was sitting behind the wheel. It was also impossible for me to read the license plate at that distance, but I noticed that the left front hubcap was missing.

I walked up the long set of steps to the front door of the apartment building where an officer was standing. I stopped and took a look up and down the street. The dark blue sedan was still parked near the corner.

"I'm Detective Nick McCord," I told the officer at the door as I pulled out my badge and ID for him to examine.

"It's apartment 3B. The manager's a little upset that we're here, but Officer Miller is standing in front of the apartment door."

"Thanks," I replied as I pulled open the door and started down the hall.

The apartment building was one of those old stucco buildings built in the early-to-mid thirties for the very wealthy. This particular apartment building had been well maintained and was still a favorite of the well-to-do. The main entrance was well lit with large glass chandeliers. The narrow halls had smaller versions of the chandeliers that were in the entrance area. The carpet was a bright red with a delicate black design running through it. The carpet was soft and quiet to walk on. The walls were plaster and painted a soft creamy off white and the wood trim was dark walnut that was polished to a bright shine. The manager's apartment was the first door on the right.

I walked up to the door and pressed the ivory colored button in the middle of the highly polished brass plate that surrounded it. The doorbell was more of a soft chime. I could hear the sound of footsteps on a hardwood floor, then the sound of the door being unlocked. The door opened and standing in front of me was a well-dressed woman in her late fifties wearing a very expensive one-piece leisure suit.

"Yes? May I help you?" she asked, as she looked me over.

"I'm Detective McCord with the police department," I said as I held out my badge and ID. "The officer at your front door tells me that you are a little upset that we have an officer in your building. I'm sorry about that, but I can assure you that it is necessary."

"I do wish you would remove your officer from the front door at least. It is very upsetting to our residents."

"I'm sorry about that, but I am investigating a murder. The officer will be staying at the door until I have had a chance to inspect Robin Flower's apartment and have it gone over by our lab people."

"Oh, my. Who was murdered?"

"Miss Robin Flower. Now do you see why it is important for me to get into that apartment?"

"Yes, certainly. I'll get a key for you."

The woman left me standing at the door while she went off to get a key. While I waited for her to return, I could see into her apartment. It was very nicely decorated in light colors and furnished in very expensive furniture

"You will return the key to me, won't you?"

"Yes, as soon as we are finished."

"You said that Miss Flower was murdered?"

"Yes, I'm afraid so," I replied.

"I am sorry to hear about Miss Flower's death. Would you be so kind as to give my condolences to her mother for me?"

"Yes, of course. Did you know Miss Flower's mother?"

"No. I never met her, but Robin often talked about her."

"Did you know Miss Flower very well?"

"Not really. We would meet in the hall or at the entrance occasionally and exchange a few words, but that was about it."

"Did you ever see her with anyone, say a boyfriend?"

"I did see her once with a tall young man. He was quite a good-looking man. I'd say he was in his late twenties, very early thirties. He looked like he might be Italian, you know, olive colored skin, dark hair, Roman nose. He was dressed very expensively. Oh, he drove one of those expensive Italian cars, I believe."

"Can you tell me if Miss Flower paid her own rent?"

"Oh, I couldn't say. Her rent was always paid by mail and always on time. We never discussed her rent."

"The envelopes would have had return addresses on them, or post marks, where were they from?"

"They were post marked here in Milwaukee, but none of the envelopes had a return address on them. I'm sure of that."

"Was her rent paid by check?" I asked.

"No. It was paid with a money order."

"Thank you, Miss - - ?"

"Mrs., Mrs. Lawrence Higgins."

"Thank you, Mrs. Higgins. I may want to talk to you again."

"I'll be around all afternoon," she replied with a smile.

I had to wonder why Robin's rent had been paid using money orders. The only reason I could think of was to make sure that no one would know who was paying the rent for the apartment. I could think of no legitimate reason to keep it a secret.

I turned and went to the stairs. Robin Flower's apartment was on the second floor. I paid very close attention to the entrances. When I turned down the hall on the second floor, I saw Officer Miller leaning against the doorframe. He immediately stood up straight when he saw me.

"Kind of boring just standing around watching a door, isn't it?"

"Yes, sir."

"Has anyone been up here since you arrived?"

"No, sir. No one has been in or out of this door."

"Okay, let's see what's inside," I said as I put the key in the lock and opened the door.

"Step inside and close the door, Miller, but don't touch anything," I instructed him.

"Yes, sir."

I stepped into the apartment with Miller right behind me. As I looked out into the living room, I heard the door close behind me. I was surprised at what I saw.

Robin's apartment was right out of <u>Good Housekeeping</u> magazine. There wasn't a thing out of place. The carpet showed signs of just having been vacuumed and there were a few magazines neatly fanned out on the coffee table as if waiting for someone to select one to read.

I walked out into the living room and looked around. I noticed that there was no indication that anyone actually lived here. It was as if I had walked into a display room just waiting for the photographer to come and take pictures. There didn't seem to be a single thing out of place.

I walked through the rest of the apartment and found it to be just like the living room, clean and neat. I found the clothes closets to be empty. Even the kitchen cupboards were empty and clean. It was as if the apartment had never been lived in. In fact, I found it was almost too clean.

"That's it," I said to myself.

"What did you say, sir?" Officer Miller asked.

"Look around, what do you see?"

I gave him a minute to look around the living room. He seemed to be puzzled by my question.

"Well?" I asked.

"I see a very expensive and very nicely decorated apartment. I know that I could never afford an apartment like this on my pay."

"It's not so much what you see as what you don't see. You don't see a speck of dust, a fresh footprint in a freshly vacuumed carpet, or a magazine out of place. This place looks as if it has never been lived in, yet it has been cleaned within the last day or so."

"I see what you mean," he replied as he looked around again.

"I would be willing to bet that we won't find a single fingerprint in the entire apartment. I want this apartment sealed off until the lab boys can go over it. I'll be back this afternoon."

"Yes, sir."

I took one last quick look around before leaving the apartment. I locked the door, then walked down the hall to the staircase. On my way out of the building I stopped by the manager's apartment and dropped off the key. I told her that I would be back later, then left the building.

As I started down the steps toward my car, I glanced down the street toward the corner. The dark blue car with the front hubcap missing was gone. I stopped. I had to wonder if I had been followed to the apartment, or if someone had just been watching the apartment house to see who was coming and going, or if I was just imagining things. One thing I knew for sure was that I had seen the dark blue car and someone was in it when I arrived. I turned and looked up at the officer standing next to the door.

"Say, did you happen to notice a dark blue sedan parked down on the corner?"

"Yes, sir. I saw it."

"Did you see it leave?"

"It left just a minute or so ago. I thought whoever was driving it should be issued a ticket."

"Why is that?"

"Because he backed around the corner and almost hit a man crossing the street. It's illegal to back around a street corner."

"Did you see the driver?"

"No, sir, but it was a man. I'm sure of that."

"Did you get a good look at the man that was almost hit?"

"No, sir. He went on around the corner. He was too far away to see very well."

"Thanks."

I glanced back toward the corner as I walked on down the steps to my car. A quick look at my watch told me I had just enough time to get to the airport and pick up Monica. The drive to the airport would give me a chance to think.

CHAPTER SIX

It took me close to an hour to drive to the airport, as the traffic was fairly heavy. By the time I found a parking space, it was a little past the scheduled arrival time for Monica's flight. As I hurried through the terminal, I kept an eye out for her. I was afraid that if her plane had arrived early, she would go to pick up any baggage that she might have checked and I might miss her.

As luck would have it, I arrived at the gate just as the passengers were beginning to come into the terminal. I waited and watched for Monica to come through the tunnel and step out into the terminal.

Suddenly, there she was. I could see her beautiful long blond hair cascading gently over her shoulders, her large cobalt blue eyes sparkling in the light and her face aglow with excitement as she came into the terminal. She moved with the grace and smoothness of a soft kitten looking for someone to pet her as her long legs moved her toward me.

As she stepped past the end of the chrome railing, she dropped her bag and threw her arms around my neck pressing her firm body against me. I wrapped her shapely body in my arms as she planted a kiss on my lips that seemed to stop all sense of anything else. It was a long hard passionate kiss that caused my whole body to respond.

"God, it's good to see you," she said breathlessly as she leaned back slightly and looked up at me.

"I missed you, too. Let's get out of here," I said, impatient to be alone with her.

I reached down and picked up her bag. She slid her arm around behind me and leaned against my shoulder as we walked down the concourse toward luggage pickup. She hung onto me as we waited for her suitcase to show up on the luggage carousel.

After getting her suitcase, we walked to the parking lot. We didn't say much. It seemed to be enough just to be together again.

After putting her luggage in the trunk, we got in. Before I could get the keys in the ignition, she leaned over, slipped her hand behind my head and pulled me toward her. Our lips met in another passionate kiss.

As she pulled back, she looked at me with a soft almost contented smile and a sparkle in her eyes.

"You are a rat," she said, but she didn't let go of me.

"What?"

"You are a rat," she repeated.

"Now just how do you figure that?"

"You had to wait until you needed me before you would call me. I should have refused to come. I should have played hard to get."

"You could have done that, but if you had I would have had to come to you," I said as casually as I could.

"Would you really have come to me?" she asked playfully.

"Of course. I need your help."

"But do you need me?"

"More than you know, much more than you know," I said as I looked into those beautiful eyes of hers.

She looked into my eyes, slowly leaned toward me and kissed me. At that rate, I could have spent the entire day right there in the airport parking structure.

When I was finally able to catch my breath, I reached down, turned the key and started the car. Once we were out on the highway and headed back toward town, I filled her in on the case I was working on. I told her about the apartment and about the brooch that had been found on Robin's body. I even told her about the Angelini family.

"It sounds as if the Angelini family is a real pillar of the community," she said with a sarcastic tone in her voice. "Have you given any thought that the family may not have liked the idea that their only son was going out with a girl that they probably considered to be beneath their status?"

"Yes, I've thought of that. But I understand that the old man loves his son more than life itself. I don't think he would kill Robin to get rid of her. He might try to buy her off, but I don't think that he would have had her killed."

"Let's take a look at this from a different point of view. Let's say that she was not killed by the Angelini family, then who would want her killed?" Monica asked.

"That I can't answer."

"Where are we going now?"

"I thought I would take you to my apartment. While you get settled in, I would go back to Robin's apartment and give it a good going over."

"If it has been cleaned as well as you say it has, what makes you think you'll find anything there that would help?" she asked.

"Something may have been overlooked. I won't be satisfied until I know for sure."

"Can I go with you? I could help you look."

I thought about her suggestion for a minute. She was not experienced in searching a house, but it certainly could not hurt anything. I doubted that there would be any fingerprints that she could ruin, I was sure that the apartment had been wiped clean.

I glanced over at her. It was easy to see that she was hoping that I would agree to let her go along.

"Sure. Why not?"

A big smile came over her face as she reached over and put her hand on my knee. I turned off the interstate and headed toward the Kilbourn Park District.

I pulled up in front of the apartment building and got out of the car. As Monica got out, she looked up at the building.

I took her hand and we walked up the steps to the front door. I couldn't help but notice the way the officer at the front door looked at Monica, but then I couldn't blame him, either.

"Have the lab boys been here yet?"

The officer quickly turned and looked at me and said, "No, sir. Not yet."

"Have them come in as soon as they get here."

"Yes, sir."

Before entering the apartment building, I glanced down the street toward the corner. I guess I was expecting to see the dark blue sedan again, but it was not there. I held the door for Monica and followed her into the building.

We stopped at the manager's apartment to get the key to Robin's apartment then went directly to the apartment. Officer Miller was still standing in front of the door. Without a word, he stepped aside and I unlocked the door.

Stepping into the room, Monica stopped and looked around. It was easy to see that the expensive decor and the neatness of the living room had impressed her.

"You weren't kidding when you said this place looked like a showroom," she said as she walked out into the living room. "It's immaculate, not a thing out of place."

"A little too immaculate, don't you think?"

"Yes, I agree. I don't know how you expect to find anything here."

"I'm hoping that whoever cleaned the place missed something."

"Good luck."

The tone of her voice and the way she said "Good luck" just reinforced my belief that there was little chance of finding anything that would be of interest. But even without much of a chance of finding anything, I still had to look.

"Here, put these on," I said as I handed her a pair of rubber gloves.

She put them on while I put on a pair. I started with the first chair I came to. I tipped it up and looked under it. It was clear that the furniture had been moved when the room was vacuumed. After setting the chair back down, I removed the cushion and carefully ran my hand down along the bottom. It was where I always seem to lose my loose change. I found nothing, not even a dime or a hair pen. It was so clean that I was sure that it had been vacuumed out when the room was cleaned.

I looked over at Monica and found her doing the same thing to another chair. We checked the sofa together and came up with nothing, not even a little lint. We continued to check everything in the room, including behind the pictures. Nothing.

"Nothing here," I said, as I looked around the room hoping for something, anything that might help.

It was clear that Monica was disappointed, but so was I. Whoever had cleaned this room had done a better job than any house cleaning service I had ever met.

"I'll take the kitchen," Monica suggested.

"Okay, I'll take the bedroom. By the way, where do women hide things in a bedroom?"

Monica smiled, "That depends on what they are hiding."

"Brooches, rings, jewelry, that sort of thing."

"Any number of places. Behind a mirror, in the bottom of draws, in a secret drawer, or under a tray inside a jewelry box. Would you like me to search the bedroom?" she asked.

"Sure. I'll take the kitchen."

While Monica headed for the bedroom, I went into the kitchen and began going through cabinets and drawers one by one. It felt strange to search an apartment that appeared to have never been lived in. It was almost as if the place had just been built, but I knew better. The cupboards were completely empty and the drawers were empty, too. They showed almost no sign that anything had ever been in them. The refrigerator was as clean as the day it was purchased, even the stove was spotlessly clean. Except for a few scratches from pans on the burners, the stove looked as if it had never been used.

As I stared at the stovetop and my mind was trying to figure out what was going on, I spotted something. It appeared to be a tiny piece of paper sticking out from under one of the spill pans under one of the back burners. I was so surprised to find anything out of place that I just stared at it for several seconds before making a move to retrieve it.

When I lifted the burner and removed the spill pan, I could see just the corner of an envelope. I replaced the spill pan and burner then lifted the top of the stove. Lying under the top of the stove was a small white envelope. I wanted to pick it up and examine it more closely, but I did not want to damage any fingerprints that might be on it even though I had gloves on. I bent down and read the address on the envelope. It was addressed to Mrs. Rose Flower, Robin's mother. There was no return address on the envelope. This was one piece of evidence that I wanted to see as soon as the lab got done with it.

"Nick, Nick. I found something you might like to see," Monica called from the bedroom.

I closed the top of the stove and went to the bedroom to see what it was that Monica had found. When I entered the bedroom, I found her kneeling on the floor in front of a freestanding jewelry chest, the large kind that sets on the floor and has eight or nine draws in it.

"What did you find?" I asked as I knelt down beside her.

Monica didn't say a word. She just looked at me as I looked down toward the floor. It seems that the jewelry chest had a hidden drawer in the bottom that looked like part of the base. She tilted the chest back a little and pulled the drawer open. Inside were several pieces of jewelry that looked to be quite valuable, and very old. One piece looked like it might match the brooch that was found on Robin's clothing.

"Great work. What do you think?"

"Some of this is very old and probably worth a lot of money. For example, this necklace," she said as she pointed at a necklace that had a hand carved ivory figure on it. "This looks like it might be from Italy and that it might be a hundred years old or older. I can't tell for sure until I examine it more closely."

"What about the rest?"

"The pin with the crest on it looks like it might be from Italy, too. The crest looks like it might be a family crest."

I reached down and picked up the pin with the crest on it. Monica looked at me with surprise.

"I don't want this one to end up in the evidence room and then disappear. I got a feeling whose family crest this might be."

I slipped the pin into my pocket, then took out a small note pad from my jacket pocket and asked Monica to make notes of the other pieces of jewelry so that we could identify them later.

She immediately began sketching each piece of jewelry on the pad. While she sketched and made notes, I looked around the bedroom. My mind was full of questions, some which could only be answered by Frank Angelini or his son, Tony. I had to wonder if Frank had this place gone over and cleaned in an effort to protect his son from being questioned about the death of Robin. During my previous run-in with Frank Angelini, I became convinced that he loved his family and would do anything to protect them. And I do mean anything.

Suddenly, I noticed something on the floor at the edge of one of the legs of the bed. It was a little round piece of paper like those made by a paper punch. It was light blue in color, and almost matched the color of the carpet. I reached down, picked it up and examined it closely. It was a piece of confetti.

I remembered that Jerry had said that a piece of confetti had been found in Robin's hair, and that the contents of her stomach had indicated that she might have been at a party only a few hours before she died. I had to wonder if the party had been here and she had actually died here, or had she been to a party somewhere else and had returned here before she was killed.

My thoughts were suddenly disturbed by the sounds of someone coming into the apartment. Monica looked at me as if waiting for instructions.

"Close that drawer and don't say anything about it, about anything," I said in a whisper as I took off the rubber gloves.

"What about the jewelry? I'm not finished."

"Forget it for now," I answered as I walked out of the bedroom toward the living room.

"Well, if it isn't the great Lieutenant Brooks. What brings you out from under your rock?"

"I'd be careful what you say. You're in enough trouble with Sinclair as it is."

"I seriously doubt that."

Just then, Monica came out of the bedroom and walked up beside me. I noticed that she had taken off the gloves. She looked at Lieutenant Brooks, then glanced up at me.

"Well, who do we have here?" Brooks said with a grin as he gave Monica the once over. "Bringing a date with you while on an investigation. How romantic, and how so against regulations. I'll have to have a talk with Captain Sinclair about this," Brooks said with a grin.

"You can talk your damn fool head off for all I care, Brooks. What are you doing here anyway?"

"You're not going to introduce me to this lovely creature?"

"First of all, I am not a creature, I am a woman," Monica stated flatly as she looked him in the eyes.

"Oh, I can see that."

"Excuse me, please," Monica said to Brooks as she took hold of my arm and looked up at me.

"I need a little refreshing here. Could this possibly be the arrogant, conceited, pompous ass, Lieutenant Brooks, you told me about?" she asked as she looked up at me.

I could not remember telling her anything about Lieutenant Brooks except that he had caused me to lose a case. She was apparently more perceptive than I had given her credit for, but then she was a very smart lady. I could hardly restrain myself from laughing out loud.

"Yes. The very same one."

"You might think this is funny now, but wait until this case gets turned over to me. Then we'll see who's laughing."

"Well until it does, you get your nose out of here and out of my business."

Brooks looked at me for a moment or two before he turned on his heels and left. Just as Brooks was leaving, Jerry and one other man from the lab came into the living room. I noticed that Jerry seemed to take a degree of satisfaction in seeing Brooks leave in a huff.

"Say, Nick. What did you do to upset our infamous Lieutenant Brooks?"

"I didn't do anything."

"Who's your new partner?" Jerry said as he looked at Monica.

"Jerry, this Monica Barnhart. Monica, Jerry Kowalski. Jerry is the Medical Examiner and the head man in the lab."

"Nice to meet you," Monica said as she stuck out her hand.

"My pleasure," he replied as he shook her hand. "Oh, this is Bob Wray. He's helping me in the lab and is excellent at finding things that people unknowingly leave behind.

"Bob, why don't you start in the kitchen?"

Jerry did not move from in front of me, but waited and watched as Bob went into the kitchen. Jerry's observation of Bob as he left the room interested me. It was almost as if he didn't trust Bob and wanted him out of the room before talking to me.

"Nick, I'm sure you've already been over the apartment. If you found anything, bring it to me when no one else is around," Jerry said, keeping his voice down.

"What's up?"

"I don't know, but Bob just came to me this morning with instructions that I was to have him "help" me with my work on any evidence involving the Robin Flower murder."

"Really? Who assigned him to work with you?"

"Captain Sinclair, as far as I know."

"Then what's the problem?"

"I don't know if you know this, or if Captain Sinclair even knows it, but Bob worked out of the West Park Division until yesterday. I made a call to a friend there. Rumor has it that he is a good friend of Brooks," Jerry said as he glanced toward the kitchen.

I found that bit of information to be very interesting. My first thought was that Captain Sinclair might be somehow involved, but I found that hard to swallow. I'd known Joe for too many years to even consider him to be a party to anything that was not on the up and up.

"Take a look around. This place has been swept clean," I said.

"Yeah, I see that."

"But not so clean that I couldn't find this."

I reached into my pocket and handed Jerry the small piece of confetti. Jerry looked at it for a second or so, then looked at me.

"If you compare this with the confetti you found in Robin's hair, I'd be willing to bet that it is the same kind of confetti."

"That doesn't prove much, Nick. There are tons of this stuff made every year."

"But it will prove that she was here after the party, or that the party was held here," I suggested.

"That's true," Jerry replied nodding his head in agreement. "I'll see what I can find and let you know."

"I also found an envelope in the kitchen. It's under the top of the strove. I didn't want to touch it until you had a chance to dust it for prints."

"I'll get it."

"Thanks, Jerry. I'd appreciate it if you would keep anything you find between us as much as you can."

"Sure."

I took Monica by the arm and led her out of the apartment. She didn't say anything until we were out of the building and standing next to the car.

"Nick, why didn't you tell him about the secret drawer in the jewelry chest?"

"Did you get all your sketches finished?"

"No."

"If Jerry doesn't find the jewelry in that secret drawer, we'll come back and finish the sketches later. I kept the key to the apartment."

"Oh," she replied with a smile.

Monica turned and got into the car. As I closed the door for her, I glanced back up toward the front of the apartment building. The officer at the front door was watching us, but turned and looked down the street when he caught me looking at him.

I walked around to the other side of my car and got in. As I started the car, I noticed a dark blue sedan parked on the other side of the street near the corner. When it pulled away from the curb and turned the corner, I couldn't see if the front hubcap was missing.

"It seems that Lieutenant Brooks has a great deal of interest in this apartment building."

"What makes you say that?"

"I just saw him drive away. He was parked at the corner behind us."

"Are you sure it was him?"

That was an interesting question. As a matter of fact, I was not sure it was him. The police department had a number of dark blue sedans used by detectives and other plain-clothes cops. For that matter, it could have been anyone.

"No, not for sure," I replied as I pulled away from the curb. "But it looked like the same car I saw at the corner earlier today."

CHAPTER SEVEN

As I drove across town toward my apartment, I kept thinking about what Monica had said. If it was not Lieutenant Brooks in the dark blue sedan, then who was it? The more I thought about it, the more I realized that it could be just about any police officer from any precinct. After all, the department had a number of dark blue sedans as well as cars of other colors. In fact, the car might not have been a police car at all, and the man inside might not have been a policeman. It was the type of car that could belong to almost anyone. The fact that it was such a plain ordinary looking car is what made it stand out.

It was after five by the time we got to my apartment. I parked the car in the garage, got out and opened the trunk. After I retrieved Monica's luggage, we climbed the three flights of stairs to my apartment. As I set her suitcase down and unlocked the door, I began to wonder if she would like my small one bedroom apartment. I swung the door open, picked up her suitcase and waited for her to enter.

I followed her into the apartment watching her face for some kind of a reaction. I wanted her to like my place, but was afraid it would not be nice enough for her.

Monica stepped inside and looked around the living room. A slight smile came over her face. I wondered what she was thinking, but I didn't have long to wait before I found out.

"This is definitely a man's apartment," she said as she placed her overnight case on a chair.

"Is that good or bad?" I asked, a little worried about what the answer might be.

"Oh, neither, really. It's just that it lacks a woman's touch, that's all. I do have to say that I like what you've done with it."

"Thank you. I spent some time this morning getting it cleaned up," I admitted.

"It's nice, really. It's very comfortable, homey in fact. I like that," she said as she turned toward me.

I set her suitcase down and pushed the door closed behind me. Monica stepped up to me, reached out and put her arms around my neck. I wrapped my arms around her narrow waist and pulled her to me.

"I've missed you," I whispered.

"I've missed you, too."

I leaned down as she tipped her face up to me. Our lips met in a warm, tender kiss. It was not the kind of kiss that evokes passion, but rather a warm loving kiss that reassured us that we loved each other and it was right for us to be together. It felt good to have her body back in my arms again and to be holding her close to me.

I leaned back and looked down at her. Her cobalt blue eyes sparkling up at me, and a soft smile came over her face. I could see a little glint in her eye that told me she had something on her mind.

"Okay, what's going on in that pretty head of yours?"

"Nothing," she replied as she nestled up against me.

"Come on. You've got something on your mind. What is it?"

"What are we going to do tonight?" she asked as she kissed me under the ear.

"Mmmmmm. I thought we might go out and get something to eat, then come back here and spend a quiet evening getting reacquainted," I suggested.

"How about we find something to eat here and start getting reacquainted right now," she suggested in that soft sexy voice I always liked to hear.

I couldn't argue with that. I had spent many a night thinking about this woman. Now that I had her in my arms again, I would be more than happy to just hang onto her.

"That suits me just fine, except for one thing. I don't know what I have in the refrigerator to eat."

"Let's find out, together. That is unless, of course, you are afraid of what I might find in the refrigerator."

"Like what?"

"You know, like those little crawly things so many bachelors have in their refrigerators from leaving food around too long."

"I am crushed, I'm absolutely crushed," I said as I tried to look dejected.

"Oh, come on. Let's see what you have," she said with a laugh in her voice.

Monica took her arms from around my neck and took hold of my hand. Together, we walked out to the kitchen. She let go of my hand and opened the door of the refrigerator. I couldn't help smiling as her face lit up with surprise. The refrigerator was well stocked with a variety of different foods, and the refrigerator was clean.

"I'm impressed. Did you do this just for me?"

"I'm sorry to say, no. I happen to enjoy cooking, and I happen to be a very good cook. I also like a clean kitchen to cook in."

"I'm impressed. You have all kinds of things to eat in here."

"Might I make a suggestion? That is, after I get a well deserved and meaningful apology."

"I'm sorry," she whispered softly. "What is your suggestion?"

"How about a nice T-bone steak with a side salad made with lettuce, tomatoes and a couple of kinds of cheese?"

"Now that sounds great."

"Good. Why don't you get settled in and make yourself comfortable while I fix dinner."

Monica leaned toward me and gave me a light kiss on the cheek, then turned and walked back toward the living room. I hesitated for a few seconds as I thought about her being here with me. Somehow, it almost didn't seem real. I had a tough time wondering what she saw in me. After all, with her looks she could be with anyone she wanted. I was just glad that she wanted to be with me.

I took a couple of steaks from the refrigerator as well as the makings for the salad. After preparing the salad, I prepared the steaks to be broiled in the oven. I hadn't heard a sound from Monica so I wasn't sure what she was doing or when she would be ready to eat. As I turned around to go check on her, I found her standing in the doorway watching me.

"You ready for me to put the steaks on?"

"Sure, I'm starving. What can I do to help?"

"You can set the table, if you like. Everything else is ready. All I need to know is how you like your steak and what kind of dressing you want on your salad."

"I like my steak medium rare and Ranch or Roquefort on the salad, if you have it."

"Great. I have both."

While I cooked the steaks and helped Monica find the dishes, she set the table. As soon as dinner was ready, we sat down and ate our meal. We talked about what she was doing at the University of Wisconsin, what she had been doing since we had last seen each other, and about what the museum had done with the jewelry recovered from Gill's Point Lodge.

It was the mention of the jewelry that reminded me of the two pieces of jewelry that I wanted her to examine. She had already seen the one piece with the family crest on it, but she had not seen the one that had been found on Robin Flower's clothing. I decided not to mention that just yet, at least not until we had finished dinner.

After dinner was over, I gathered up the dirty dishes and placed them on the counter. While I cleared the remaining salad and dressings from the table, Monica began running water into the sink.

"What are you doing?" I asked, a little surprised that she would jump right in to clean up the kitchen.

"I thought we could wash up the dishes while we talk about this case you're working on."

"Okay," I replied as I picked up a dish towel.

"Like I already told you, it looks a lot like the Angelini family is very much involved in the death of Robin Flower, but it doesn't seem to make any sense. There were a number of people connected with the family, in one way or another, at the park on the afternoon that Robin's body was found. It was almost as if they were having a family reunion, or a gathering of the clan," I said as I slowly dried a plate.

"It doesn't sound much like you believe that the Angelini family is really involved in the death of the girl."

I looked at her as I thought about what she had said, and saw her holding out another plate for me to dry. The look on her face told me that she was trying to get me to come up with other possibilities. I put away the plate I had been drying for the past several minutes and took the one she held out for me.

"That has crossed my mind," I admitted.

"What has?" she asked.

"That the Angelini family isn't involved in the death of Robin. Let's say that the Angelini family isn't involved, not that they wouldn't kill someone if they thought it was necessary to protect the family. That leaves us with a number of unanswered questions.

"For example, what were so many of Frank Angelini's people, his enforcers and bodyguards, doing in the park that afternoon?"

"Was Frank Angelini in the park?" she asked.

"Not that we know of. In fact, it was rumored that Frank has been ill and hasn't been out of the house for several weeks."

"Then there has to be another reason for them to be in the Park," she said thoughtfully.

"Sure," I replied. "But what? Not one of them lives anywhere near the South Shore Park. They all live on the other side of town. Even Robin lived on the other side of town."

"Maybe, you're looking too hard for a connection to the Angelini family, when there isn't one," Monica suggested.

I put the plate away and looked at Monica. She was busy scrubbing the broiler pan. Slowly, she turned and glanced up at me. She had a puzzled look on her face.

"What?" she asked.

"Oh, there's a connection all right, and I think I've just figured out what it might be. Listen to this and tell me what you think.

"Let's say that no one connected to the Angelini family committed the murder of Robin Flower."

"Okay," she replied as she stopped to listen to me.

"Just suppose that someone wanted to make a hit against the Angelini family that would hurt them bad, while trying to avoid a direct attack against the family itself. At the same time, they're trying to make it look like someone close to the family was involved. This would get the police snooping into what the family is doing by questioning those close to the family. Having the police snooping around is not something Frank Angelini would like."

"I suppose that's possible, but why?" she asked.

"That I don't know, but there are any number of reasons. It could be that someone wants to make the Angelini family aware of the fact that they are vulnerable. Possibly, it's someone who is seeking revenge for something a member of the Angelini family did to him or to one of his or her family members.   Possibly, someone from another crime family wants the Angelini family out of the way."

"Or possibly, it was just plain jealousy," Monica added.

That was one possibility that I had not thought of, but it was definitely a possibility.

"How did they get so many of the people connected with the family in the park at the same time?" Monica asked.

Monica had a very good point. I had to think about that for a minute.

"Someone had to arrange it. It had to be someone that they all trusted, or at least someone they all knew," I said thoughtfully.

"You said that you had a broach that you wanted me to look at," Monica reminded me as she interrupted my thoughts.

"Oh, yes. It's in the bedroom."

"Why don't you get it while I finish up here? I'll be done in a minute."

I hated to leave her to finish up, but there was only the table and counter to wipe off. After putting my dishtowel on the towel rack, I left her in the kitchen while I went to the bedroom to retrieve the broach and the pin with the family crest on it. Monica had just put the dishcloth over the towel rack and was wiping her hands when I returned to the kitchen.

"Here you are. What do you think of this?" I asked as I handed her the broach.

Monica looked over the broach that had been taken from the clothing of Robin Flower. She first examined one side then rolled it over in her hand to examine the other side. She painstakingly examined every minute detail of the latch and catch, the tiny prongs that held the ivory carved figure in place and every detail of the delicately carved figure.

"This is very old, probably a hundred or more years old. It has all the characteristics of being handmade, probably in Italy. The Ivory is most likely from an African elephant, but that I can't be sure of without taking it to the lab for a more detailed study."

"Is the figure carved in the ivory of someone, or is it just a figure?"

"I can't say for sure, but I believe it is of some individual who was important to whoever had this made, or to whoever it was made for."

Still looking at it, she made a soft almost inaudible sound. I looked at her, wondering what she might have found.

"Do you have a magnifying glass?"

"Yes, I think so," I replied as I stood up.

I went into the living room and rummaged through my desk until I found it under some papers. I returned to the kitchen with the magnifying glass and handed it to her. She turned the broach upside down and began carefully studying the back of it.

"Look here," she said as she handed me the magnifying glass and pointed to a small part of the back of the broach.

I took the glass and examined the area of the broach that she had pointed out for me. It wasn't clear to me at first just what I was looking for, but I soon noticed some writing. I couldn't read all of it, but it appeared to be a name and something else. However, there was one word that wasn't too hard to read under the magnifying glass. It was "Angelini".

"Do you know what the rest of this says?"

"It's the mark of the jeweler who made it and who it was made for. This broach was made sometime between eighteen-fifteen and eighteen-forty, and it was made for one of the members of the Angelini family, probably a great-grandfather," Monica said.

"It's not likely that the Angelini family would let this out of the family. It's a family heirloom. I find it hard to believe that Frank Angelini would let Tony give the broach to his girl friend," I said as I turned and looked at Monica.

"Well, if Frank Angelini loves his son as much as you say he does, he might let him do it," Monica suggested. "Especially if the old man liked Robin and he was convinced that his son was going to marry her."

"My guess would be that Frank doesn't know that Tony gave the broach to Robin."

"You might be right," Monica said as she picked up the pin with the family crest on it.

I watched her as she examined the small delicate pin, using the magnifying glass. She rolled the pin over in her hand as she carefully scrutinized every minute detail of it.

"This pin was made by the same jeweler as the broach."

"Does it say on the back who it was made for?"

"No, it's too small for that. But the crest is defiantly Italian. I don't think it's the Angelini family crest."

"What makes you say that?"

"I think the tiny letter in the center of the crest is a "C" not an "A". It's very hard to see with the naked eye since it is so small, and hard to make out with the fancy script. Usually that's the first letter of the last name of the family. I think Sam Kishler at the university might be able to tell us whose crest it is. We can photograph it, have it enlarged and send it to him in the morning."

"Okay," I agreed.

"Do you think it might have been passed down to the Angelini family from one of the women who married into the family?"

"If it belongs to Frank Angelini now, that is very likely. It could be the family crest of Frank's mother or grandmother. Sam might be able to tell us."

Monica handed the pin and broach to me. I wanted to put them in a safe place. If the Angelini family found out that I had them, they might try to get them back without asking politely.

I went to my bedroom and stood just inside the doorway. I slowly looked around the room trying to think of a safe place to hide the jewelry. I thought about putting them in my closet, but that would be the first place anyone would look. In the dresser was no better a place to hide them. Then it hit me; I could pin them both to the fabric on the bottom of the seat cushion on the antique wooden chair that sat in the corner of the bedroom. They would be out of sight and no one would suspect that there was anything under the seat.

I had not noticed what Monica had done with her luggage until this very minute. I noticed that she had her suitcase sitting on the chair in the corner. It was open and a robe was laid out over the back of the chair.

"I hope you don't mind. After all, you did say to make myself at home."

I turned around and saw Monica standing behind me, watching me. I smiled at her, "Not at all. I was just trying to decide where to hide the jewelry. I think I'll hide it under this chair."

"That looks like a good place."

After I moved Monica's suitcase to the bed, she took her robe from the chair. I tipped the chair over and carefully pinned the jewelry in the folds of the material on the bottom of the seat. Setting the chair back on its legs, I put her suitcase back on the chair.

"There, that should keep them safe for a little while."

"What now?" Monica asked.

"Well, I think it's time to relax and forget about this case for a little while. I would like very much to get reacquainted with you."

Monica stepped up to me, put her hands on my shoulders and looked into my eyes. I reached out, put my hands on her narrow waist and drew her close to me.

"You know what I've missed most?" she asked in a soft whisper.

"No."

"I've missed having you hold me," she said as she looked into my eyes.

I smiled then gently pulled her closer. I wrapped my arms around her as our lips met in a hard passionate kiss. Her soft hands slipped around behind my head as she pressed her body against me. I don't know how long the kiss lasted, but I knew that she was all the woman I would ever need. She was beautiful, passionate, loving and intelligent.

She leaned back and looked up at me. "If you don't mind, I would like to take a shower."

"I don't mind at all. The news will be on in a few minutes and I would like to watch it."

"I'll be out in a minute."

I gave Monica a light kiss, then left the bedroom. After getting a cup of coffee, I sat down in front of the television and turned it on. It would be a little while before the news came on, so I watched the last few minutes of a movie while I waited.

In the background, I could here the water running in the bathroom. My mind wondered off to another time when I had been with Monica. Here I was with a beautiful, sexy woman in my apartment, and I wanted to watch the news. I must be crazy.

It wasn't so much that I wanted to watch the news as it was a case of wanting to find out how much the news media knew about Robin Flower's murder. I found out a long time ago that the news has ways of finding out things you would prefer they didn't know, and sometimes, knew things you wished that you knew.

Monica came into the living room just as the news was starting. She was wearing a delicate lacy robe that contoured to the smooth flowing lines of her body.

"Are you trying to distract me from the news?" I asked, as I looked her over.

"I would be very disappointed if I could not distract you from almost anything in this robe. It was expensive and I bought it especially for you," she replied as she moved gracefully across the room toward the sofa.

She sat down beside me on the sofa and curled her legs under herself. Leaning against me, I could feel the warmth of her body and smell the fresh sent of her soap from her shower.

I rested my hand on her knee as she reached behind me and gently rubbed the back of my neck. I was more than willing to give up the news and was about to tell her so when the news anchorman's words penetrated my thoughts.

" - - - - Robin Flower was found dead on the beach at South Shore Park. Although the cause of death has not yet been released by the police department, our sources tell us that Miss Flower died from an overdose of cocaine."

I was surprised to hear that his sources had told him about the cocaine. Those who had been on the beach were sure that the cause of death had been from a gunshot wound to the back of the head.

On the television screen was a well-dressed and rather handsome man talking into a microphone. It was clear that he was standing on the beach with Lake Michigan as his backdrop.

"This is the place where Miss Flower's body was found. We have with us tonight, Lieutenant Brooks from the West Park Division of the Milwaukee Police Department," the newsman said as Brooks stepped into the camera's view.

It was easy for me to see who the newsman's source was in this case. With one of his men in the lab, Brooks would be able to get first hand information and leak to the press what he wanted them to know.

"It is our understanding that you are leading up the investigation in this case."

"Well, let's just say that I'm involved in it," Brooks replied with a smile.

"You sure as hell are, I just can't figure out how," I said more to myself than to Monica.

"Are there any suspects in the case?"

"As of right now, we don't have very much to go on. It will most likely be a long, drawn out investigation. We have a number of leads, but I can't discuss them at this time."

"Thank you, Lieutenant Brooks," the newsman said."

"He sure likes the news media, doesn't he?" Monica said.

"He does like to be in the limelight."

"What do you say we shut off the television and spend a little time on us?"

"Are you trying to distract me from my duties as a detective?"

"I sure am," she replied as she leaned over and kissed me lightly on the lips.

"I think I'll take my shower."

"I'll wait for you in bed, if you don't mind."

"I don't mind at all."

After switching off the television, I stood up and reached out to Monica. She took my hand and stood up. We walked into the bedroom together, then I went on into the bathroom.

It didn't take me long to shower and shave. When I returned to the bedroom, I found Monica waiting for me in the bed. The robe she had been wearing was hung over the back of the chair in the corner.

"Coming?" she asked softly as she held up the covers inviting me to join her under them.

I moved over to the bed, sat down on the edge and rolled in under the covers. She covered me as she rolled up against me, then wrapped her arms around me. I could feel the warmth of her bare breasts as she moved closer to kiss me. It was only a matter of seconds before I had forgotten everything outside the bedroom.

Her skin was soft and smooth, yet her body was firm against mine. I slide my hand up the smooth skin of her side and over one of her breasts. The feel of her naked body under my hands was exciting.

Our passion for each other grew quickly. Our bodies became as one as our passion and desire for each other overtook us. It wasn't long before we were lost in our love for each other.

CHAPTER EIGHT

I don't know if it was the sound of the thunder and the rain outside my window that woke me, or if it was Monica as she rolled over on her side next to me. Either way, I opened my eyes and found the room to be darker than usual. I wondered what time it might be.

Rolling over, I reached across Monica to turn the clock so that I could see the time. My hand never reached the clock. Monica took hold of my hand and wrapped my arm around her as she pressed my hand against one of her firm, warm breasts. She murmured softly as she snuggled back against me.

"You feel good," she whispered softly.

"So do you," I replied as I drew her tightly up against me.

The feel of her warm back against my chest, her firm shapely butt against my stomach and her long legs against mine made me feel so calm that I found it easy to relax and doze off again. I could think of no better place to be than curled up against this warm beautiful woman as I closed my eyes and drifted off to sleep.

* * * *

The second time I woke, I found myself still holding onto her. I could feel the softness of her hand as she gently rubbed my arm. It was impossible for me to tell what was going on in her mind, but I liked waking up with Monica wrapped in my arms and curled up against me.

I gently squeezed her breast to let her know I was awake. She murmured softly, then lifted my hand to her lips and kissed it. Rolling over on her back, she looked over at me and smiled.

"Good morning," she said as she stretched, the sheet clinging to the smooth curved lines of her body.

"Good morning. Are you hungry?" I asked.

"Yes. I'm starving after last night," she said with a knowing smile.

I leaned over to her and kissed her lightly on the lips.

"Give me a couple of minutes, then you can have the bathroom while I fix us something to eat."

I rolled away from her and sat up on the edge of the bed for a second. She reached out and touched my back with the tips of her fingers. I looked back over my shoulder and smiled at her.

"I like it when you touch me, too, but if you keep that up, you won't get any breakfast."

"I guess I better quit," she said softly.

"I'll be out shortly," I said as I stood up and walked into the bathroom.

After a quick shower, I dressed and went out to the kitchen to fix breakfast. I heard the shower running and smiled to myself at the thought of her standing in the shower with fresh clean water cascading over her naked body. I had a sudden urge to join her, but decided against it.

Instead, I decided to fix eggs with English muffins and orange juice. While I was preparing the eggs, I reached up in the cupboard for the salt when I noticed a container of tea with a small red fox on the label. The fox reminded me of the man that Robert Goouchie had warned me about, Travis Fox.

He was the only one that I had little or no information on. His local arrest record did little to tell me about him, other than that he was a brutal man. It only hinted at what might be contained in his Chicago files. I had no idea who he worked for, what he was doing here, or why he had come here from Chicago.

"What's the matter?"

The sound of Monica's voice startled me. I turned around to see her looking at me with a very worried look on her face and fear in her eyes. The last thing I wanted to do was to cause her to worry, or to be afraid.

"I'm sorry, honey. I was just thinking about something."

"Robin's killer?" she asked as she stepped up to me.

She put her arms around my waist and laid her head on my chest. I wrapped my arms around her and held her tight.

"One of the suspects."

She didn't move. She simply squeezed me as she held onto me.

I reached down and gently took her chin in my hand and lifted her face. As I looked down into her eyes, I could see that she was concerned about me.

"I love you," I said in a tone that showed my concern for her. "And I don't want anything to happen to you. If Frank Angelini finds out that I have his family pin, he will spare none of his resources to get it back. Do you understand what I'm saying?"

Looking up at me, her eyes began to water. It was clear that she was beginning to understand.

"You want me to go back to Madison, don't you?"

"Yes. I want you to take the pin back to the university and find out everything you can about it, then call me."

"I thought we were going to send a picture of it to Sam Kishler?"

"Yes, I know. But I think it would be better if you take the pin to him. I don't want anyone to know we have it."

"You're afraid for me," she said as she looked into my eyes. "You're afraid something might happen to me, aren't you?"

"Yes," I admitted. "I am afraid for you. I don't want you involved in this case because it could get messy, very messy. We're not dealing with some small-time hood. The Angelini family is a well organized operation, and they won't stop at anything to get what they want."

Monica let go of me, stepped back and looked at me for a moment, then turned her back to me. I wanted to take her in my arms and tell her I was sorry, but her safety was more important to me than anything. I would not be able to stand it if anything happened to her.

"I really want you here with me," I tried to explain. "But it's too dangerous. Once this is over I will come to you."

Monica turned around and looked at me. Tears were running down her face. I could not stand to see her cry.

"I'm sorry. You're right. It's not fair of me to drag you into this mess, then send you away."

"Nick, I want to help you. I want to do whatever I can to help you get to the bottom of this young girl's death. Can't you understand that?"

"Yes. Yes I can. Let's have breakfast and get that picture made and sent off to Sam," I said as I stepped up in front of her and took her in my arms.

Monica laid her head on my shoulder and held onto me. Although I had given into her, it didn't change anything. I was still very worried about her.

After a few moments, Monica returned to the bathroom to wash her face while I finished fixing breakfast. We ate, then went to a nearby mall where we had pictures taken of the pin. I could have had the pictures taken in the police lab, but there were too many eyes watching me there.

We returned to my apartment after express mailing the photos along with a note to Sam Kishler at the University of Wisconsin. Just as we walked into my apartment the phone began to ring. I reached over and picked it up.

"Hello."

"Nick?"

"Yeah."

"This is Jerry. Guess who just showed up on my autopsy table this morning?"

"Who?"

"Danny Minger."

"Damn," I said more to myself than to anyone who could hear me.

"Wasn't he the guy you had hidden away for safe keeping?" Jerry asked.

"Yes. How did you know I had him hidden away?"

"Word gets around fast here."

"What was the cause of death?"

"I'm not one hundred percent sure yet, but it looks like he choked to death on something he was eating, possibly a hot dog."

"I don't believe it," I said in frustration. "See what you can find out. If you come up with anything other than "choked to death", keep it to yourself until we can talk in private."

"Right. I've got to go, someone's coming."

The phone suddenly went dead. I hung up the phone and looked at Monica.

"What's the matter?"

"One of my witnesses, Danny Minger, who I just happened to have under protective custody, is dead. It looks like someone got to him, and it had to be someone who knew where I had him hidden away."

"Are you sure? Maybe it was an accident. I did hear you say that he chocked to death."

"I'm sure. I certainly don't believe it was an accident. I don't think Jerry thinks it was an accident either or he wouldn't have called me at home when no one was in the lab."

"Do you have any idea who it might be?"

"No, not really. Jerry is going to do the autopsy on him. He will let me know what he finds."

"Can Jerry be trusted?"

"At the moment, he's about the only one I can trust, but he is being watched, too."

"What about your captain?"

"Captain Sinclair? We go back a long ways. I believe I can trust him."

"Are you sure?"

Monica's simple question made me think. I had known Joe Sinclair from as far back as when I went through the police academy. He was one of my instructors and the first officer I rode with after graduating. He taught me a lot of what I know about investigating.

After my probation was over, I was reassigned to another officer. I sort of lost track of Joe until about five years ago when I was promoted to detective and assigned to his precinct. I never spent much time with him outside the office, but he always had a good word, always seemed concerned about others, and always listened to what I had to say. I found it difficult to think that he might have had something to do with the death of Danny Minger.

"I sure hate to think that he had anything to do with this," I said as I looked up at Monica.

Monica moved over next to me and sat down. I could see in her eyes that she wished she had not mentioned it, but I was glad that she did. This was one woman who could keep me focused and help me consider all the possibilities.

"I'm sorry," she said softly. "I didn't mean to be so cold about it."

"That's okay. You got me thinking."

"About what?"

"It might be a good idea if I find out the names of everyone that knew I had Danny in the lockup."

"How will you do that?"

"I'll start with Pete Wallace,"

"Who's Pete Wallace?"

"He's a long time friend of mine who just happens to be the head jailer where I had Danny under lock and key."

"Are you sure he isn't responsible for Danny's death? You have often said that the most obvious answer to a problem is usually the right one."

"That would mean that someone got to Pete. Of all the people I know, Pete is the most honest."

I'm sorry," she said. "I don't know these people like you do. I just want you to be careful."

"I understand," I said with a smile. "I've got to have a talk with Pete. I'll be back in a little while."

Monica nodded that she understood. As I left the apartment, I waited to see if Monica would lock the door behind me. I felt much better hearing the door being locked.

I headed toward my car, which I had parked in the garage. As I stepped around the corner of the garage, I saw a large black Cadillac turning into the parking lot. Although the Cadillac interested me, it was the dark blue sedan that was parked a half a block away that really caught my attention. Even from the garage I could see that it was missing a front hubcap.

I turned my attention back to the large black Cadillac when it pulled up beside me and stopped. The dark tinted window of the backdoor slowly rolled down. Behind the window was none other than Frank Angelini himself. I was surprised to see him in person. I would have thought that he would send one of his thugs to talk to me.

"Well, well. If it isn't Frank Angelini in person, no less. What brings you to this neighborhood, Frank?"

"I want to have a little chat with you, Detective McCord," he said ignoring my comment.

"What about?"

"You know damn well what it's about. Do I have to spell it out for you?"

"Good idea, Frank. Why don't you spell it out for me."

"Somebody murdered my son's fiancée, and I want him. I know that you're working on the case."

"Just how do you know that?"

"I have my sources."

"I'll bet. I'd even be willing to bet that one of them is none other than our own Lieutenant Brooks."

I threw out Lieutenant Brooks's name just to see what sort of a response I might get. There was not a hint of any kind of change in Frank's expression or in his eyes. Either Lieutenant Brooks was not his source, or this man really knew how to keep his cool. I suspect that over the years, Frank Angelini had learned not to tip his hand in any kind of negotiations.

"What is it you really want, Frank?"

"I want to be the first to know who it was that killed the girl. I want to know before you go to arrest him. I want to save the city the time and expense of putting whoever it was on trial. Do you understand?"

"Oh, I understand all right. I think it is very generous of you to want to save the taxpayers the expense of a long trial," I said as I looked him right in the eye. "But I don't care what you want. You understand this. I'm going to find out who killed Miss Flower even if it leads me right to your front doorstep. Do you understand that?"

Frank looked at me as if he was trying to figure out what I was getting at. I got the impression that he was sure that I already had an idea of who did the killing, but he was not sure enough to ask.

Frank never took his eyes off me as the window began to slowly go up. I had to wonder what was going through his mind at that moment. I had made it clear that no matter what, I was going to find the killer. I had also made it clear that he was not going to get me to tell him anything until I was darn good and ready to do so.

I stepped back slightly as the car began to move. I watched as the Cadillac sped off down the drive then turn out onto the street. It was at that moment that I remembered the dark blue sedan parked down the block. I quickly turned around in time to see the sedan pull away from the curb and turn down an alley. It looked as if there were two people in the car this time, but it was too far away for me to see who they were.

I stood there for a moment or two thinking before I opened the garage door. Seeing the sedan pull away like it did caused me to wonder if whoever was in the car was following Angelini, or if they were watching me. The fact that they drove off when Angelini drove away made me think that they might be following Angelini. However, I'd seen that car around too many times to keep that thought for very long.

I got in my car and drove down to the police station. I must admit that I kept my eyes open to see if I was being followed. I saw no one that I could honestly say was following me. When I turned into the police garage and parked my car, I noticed three dark blue sedans parked in a neat row in spaces reserved for police cars.

I smiled to myself and shook my head as I started to walk toward the entrance. At this point, I was beginning to feel as if I was suffering from severe paranoia. It seemed that everywhere I looked and everywhere I went, I saw a dark blue sedan. They seemed to be all over the place. Now there were three of them right in front of me.

As I walked by the three unmarked police cars, I could not help myself. I had to look at them. At first, they all looked just alike. Suddenly, I stopped. I knew that they were not all alike. There was something very different about the second one. A closer look at the front left wheel made it very much different from the others. It was missing the left front hubcap. I was sure that it was the same car I had seen several times over the past couple of days.

I stood looking at the car for several moments trying to think of who had been driving it. I still had it in mind that the car was the one that was assigned to Lieutenant Brooks. I had to wonder why he was at this precinct. Unable to come up with a reasonable answer, I went inside.

When I arrived at my desk, I glanced up and saw Lieutenant Brooks standing in Captain Sinclair's office. The look on the captain's face gave me no clue as to what Brooks was doing here, but Brooks was apparently ready to leave.

Brooks glanced over at me with one of his self-satisfied grins as he started to leave the Captain's office. It was that grin that gave me the clue as to why he was here. There was no doubt in my mind that he had reported to Captain Sinclair that I had a date with me while I was working on a case, namely Monica.

Captain Sinclair followed Brooks out of his office and then turned toward me. I watched him as he approached my desk.

"How's it going, Nick?"

"Not bad, Captain. What's Brooks doing over here? Is he looking for another apology?"

"Does he have one coming?"

"Not from me."

"Well, for your information, he was here to tell me about the woman you had with you at Robin Flower's apartment yesterday. Since when do we take civilians with us on an investigation without approval?" he asked, the stern look on his face telling me that he was serious and that I had better have a good explanation.

"Sorry about that, Captain, but Doctor Barnhart is with the history department of the University of Wisconsin. She's an expert on antique jewelry."

He looked a little confused so I explained to him that I had picked her up at the airport shortly before going to Robin's apartment. I explained that I had called her to help identify the broach that had been found on Robin Flower's blouse.

There was something unsettling about the way he looked at me while I explained. I couldn't put my finger on it, but he seemed more than a little surprised that I had called in an expert to help. However, he seemed to accept my explanation and let it drop there after I told him that she had come to lend her expertise without any expense to the department. I'm not sure if he actually believed me, but he turned, walked back to his office and shut the door without comment.

As I stood up and started to leave my desk, I noticed that he was on the phone. He stopped talking and watched me as I walked by his office to the elevator. I never knew him to do that before. The expression on his face as he watched me walk by gave me cause to wonder what he was thinking and who was on the other end of the phone.

I went to the elevator and took it to the basement. As I walked into the lab, I noticed Bob Wray sitting at a desk looking through some papers. He had a small pad on the desk and a pen in his hand. It looked as if he was making some notes. My sudden appearance in the lab startled him and he quickly closed the file as he looked up at me. The look on his face was like that of a small child that had been caught with his hand in the cookie jar. He looked guilty as sin, but guilty of what I had no idea.

Without giving him any indication that I had seen what he was doing, I simply asked where Jerry might be found. He said nothing. He simply pointed at the door to the autopsy room. I nodded and pushed through the door.

I found Jerry standing over the body of Danny Minger who was stretched out on the stainless steel table. Jerry had forceps in one hand and a scalpel in the other. Danny's mouth was wide open. I stood and watched as Jerry cut away a small piece of tissue from inside Danny's mouth.

"Find anything?" I asked as soon as he had removed the piece of tissue.

Jerry looked up, then looked around the room and smiled.

"More than you know," he said as he put the specimen in a small container.

"What's that mean?"

Jerry again looked around the room before speaking, making sure that no one could hear him.

"Your friend Danny didn't accidently choke to death like the guard said. He was murdered."

"Are you sure?"

"As sure as I'm standing here. It was reported that he choked to death on a piece of hot dog, which in fact he did. But this was not just any old hot dog. The hot dog...."

Jerry suddenly stopped talking when the door behind me opened. I turned around to see Bob Wray come into the room.

"As I was saying, he choked to death on a plain ordinary hot dog. My guess is that he was upset and trying to eat too fast," Jerry said flatly, as if it was the gospel truth.

It was easy for me to understand what Jerry was trying to do. It was probably for the best. After all, Jerry could be risking his life by letting out what he knew to the wrong person.

"Tough break, Nick," Bob said with a slight grin that he seemed to be having trouble keeping under control.

"Yeah, a real tough break," I replied as I watched the little weasel squirm back out the door to the outer office.

"Nick, someone injected some kind of a local anesthetic into the hot dog," Jerry whispered. "When Danny bit into the hot dog, it released the anesthetic. Within seconds, Danny couldn't feel anything and he couldn't swallow either. Results, he choked to death on the hot dog because he couldn't feel that it was still in this throat."

"You're kidding, aren't you?" I asked.

"No. When Danny bit into the hot dog, it released the anesthetic, which deadened the surface nerves in his mouth and throat much like when a dentist deadened the tissue inside your mouth before he injects a stronger anesthetic to deaden the nerve.

"Danny lost all sense of feeling in his mouth and throat almost instantly. When he tried to swallow the hot dog, he couldn't feel it. When he started to chock on it, he couldn't get it out and suffocated."

"Can you prove it?"

"Yes, but it will be difficult with Wray hanging around all the time."

"Do what you can, but be careful. I'll try to find out who gave Danny the hot dogs."

As I left the lab, I saw that Wray was on the phone. I noticed that he immediately stopped talking when I came out of the autopsy room. He waited until I was out of the office before he resumed his conversation.

I spent the next hour or so talking with several of the jailers, with the cooks who prepared the food, and with the custodian. I even spent a few minutes in the cell where Danny had been locked up, but I was unable to turn up anything out of the ordinary or anything that might lead me to who had killed him. The only thing that I was sure of was that Danny was dead and so was my lead to Travis Fox.

I found Pete Wallace in the coffee room drinking a cup of coffee. He looked up at me as I walked in.

"I'm sorry about Minger. I found out about it this morning."

"Any idea how someone got to him?"

"No. Do you think this was something more than an accident?

"Yes, but I can't prove it. Was there anyone around that usually isn't down here?"

"No," he answered. "Wait a minute. That new guy who's working in the lab was down here yesterday just before I got off."

"You mean Bob Wray?"

"Yeah, that's the guy. But he didn't go anywhere near the security cell. He wasn't even close to Minger."

"Was he in the kitchen?"

"That I can't say for sure," he replied after thinking about it for a minute.

"Thanks, Pete. Keep our talk between us," I said.

He nodded that he would, I then left.

I wondered how Wray could have gotten the anesthetic into the hot dogs that would go to Minger. How would he know which food tray to put the hot dogs on? I had no way of knowing how he would find that out.

I was getting nowhere real fast here. It was possible that Wray had done it, though I couldn't see how. As I started to leave the jail area, I remembered that the trays were marked with the cell number for those in cells by themselves. All that would be required was for Wray to pull it off was for the cooks to have their backs turned for just a couple of seconds while Wray was there.

At least that was a possible explanation of how it could be done. Even if Wray had left his fingerprints on the serving tray, it would have been washed by now eliminating them. The only problem I had was proving that Wray had tampered with the hotdogs.

There was nothing else that I could do here, at least for now. I decided to return to my apartment and make my decisions on what I was going to do next. One thing was certain, I was going to have to have a talk with Travis Fox.

CHAPTER NINE

I stopped off at my desk for a minute to pick up the file on Travis Fox. I wanted to know as much about him as possible before I questioned him. As I was leaving for the police garage, I noticed that Captain Sinclair was still talking on the phone. He had his back to me and didn't see me as I walked by on my way to my car.

As I stepped out the door into the police garage, I immediately noticed that one of the dark blue sedans was gone. Since two were still there, it was easy for me to reason that one of them had been the one Lieutenant Brooks was driving.

I could see no reason to examine the remaining cars, as I was sure that the one with the missing hubcap was already gone. However, something in the back of my mind told me that I should take a look at them anyway so that I would know for sure. I was surprised to see that the car with the missing hubcap was still there.

The surprise was so great that I just stood there looking at the car for several seconds, now more confused then ever. If Lieutenant Brooks had not been driving the car with the missing hubcap, then who had been driving it? Was it Sinclair, or someone else that I had not considered?

I took a minute to look around the police garage, but saw no one. The place was totally void of anyone. My mind was racing a mile a minute in an effort to find an answer to who had been driving the car with the missing hubcap. I turned and walked to my own car. I got in and sat down behind the wheel. I sat and stared out the windshield, thinking. I could always call the motor pool and find out who the car was assigned to. The problem with that was it would be too easy for someone to find out about an inquiry about the car.

From where my car was parked, I could see the two remaining dark blue sedans. I was hidden back in the shadows almost out of sight. I was so consumed with my thoughts that I wasn't sure why I had chosen to just sit there and stare at those two cars.

As I was reaching for the key to start my car, I saw something move out of the corner of my eye. I turned to get a better view and noticed Captain Sinclair coming out of the building. He was walking toward the dark blue sedans. I watched him to see which one of the cars he was going to take.

I felt a deep feeling of disappointment come over me as I watched him get into the dark blue sedan with the missing hubcap. My first thought was maybe Monica was right. It was sure beginning to look as if Sinclair might have some involvement in all of this after all. Yet, there was something wrong with what I was seeing.

Sinclair seemed to be having trouble with the car. It looked like he was having difficulty getting the car started. I saw him stop, look over at the other dark blue sedan, and then look back at the one he was sitting in.

Suddenly, the car door flew open and Sinclair got out of the car, slamming the door behind him. He appeared to be rather upset as he walked around to the driver's side of the other sedan, jerked opened the door and got in. Within seconds he had the car started and backed out of the parking space. As he drove away, I let out a sigh of relief. He had not been driving the one with the missing hubcap after all. He had simply gotten into it by mistake.

I suddenly realized that if Sinclair had not been driving the car with the missing hubcap, and Lieutenant Brooks had not been driving it, then who had been driving it? I sat there for the better part of fifteen minutes trying to come up with a logical answer, but there was no answer. I took a minute to jot down the license number so I could positively identify the car later by more than a missing hubcap.

I glanced at my watch and suddenly realized that it was getting on toward noon. I was sure that Monica would be getting worried about me. I started my car and drove back to my apartment.

When I arrived at my apartment, I found that Monica had lunch set out on the table. We sat down to eat. We talked about what had happened at the police station. As soon as we were done, Monica insisted that I go into the living room and go over the file on Travis Fox while she cleaned up the kitchen.

I sat down at my desk and opened the file. Slowly, page by page, I went through the file. Travis Fox was six foot two with wavy dark brown hair and brown eyes. He had no known distinguishing marks. Even the normally unflattering police photos showed that he was not at all unlikable in his appearance. He was certainly not ugly. He was one man that most women would consider rather handsome.

A study of his arrest record revealed nothing that I didn't expect to see or hadn't seen when I briefly looked through it the other night. He had been arrested several times for various crimes like, aggravated assault, assault with intent to do bodily harm, and assaulting an officer. That was just here in Milwaukee and over two years ago. There was nothing in the last eighteen months or more.

Once again, I made mental notes of the number of times that Lieutenant Brooks's name showed up in Fox's arrest record. Brooks's name showed up so often that it appeared as if Brooks was looking out for this guy, sort of protecting him, but why? What was Fox to Brooks? Better yet, what did Fox have on Brooks that would make Brooks stick his neck out to get this guy released from custody on such serious charges?

"What did you find out about your prime suspect?" Monica asked as she leaned over my shoulder to see what I was reading.

"Just enough to be very careful how I approach this guy. He seems to have a mean streak a mile wide. He doesn't seem to care who he beats up on. Twice, he vented his anger on women. One was a prostitute, the other was a woman he had invited out to dinner."

"Sounds like a real gentleman," Monica said with a note of sarcasm in her voice.

"Yeah, but here is something even stranger. He has not been arrested or even had a police contact in at least the last eighteen months."

"That does seem strange. What happened that caused the sudden change?"

"I don't know. I think I will stop and see this "gentleman" at the jewelry store where he works. I understand his uncle owns the place."

Monica was still looking over my shoulder reading the arrest record. She turned her head and looked at me.

"Why do I see Lieutenant Brooks's name on so many of the entries?"

"A very good question. One that I think deserves a very good answer," I said as I pushed back my chair.

"Where are you going now?"

"I think I will go have a little talk with Mr. Fox."

"Can I go along?"

"I don't think that's a very good idea."

"Why not? I could look around while you talk to him. I might see something that would be of interest."

The thought of Monica in the same room with anyone as violent as Fox would tend to make me nervous. Yet, on the other hand, she might have a good point. Just by being in the store, she could observe his reaction to my visit. With a great deal of reluctance, I agreed to take her with me.

"Okay, you can come along, but I want you to do something for me. I want you to give me a few minutes in the store before you come in, then stay a few minutes after I leave. I want to know what he does as soon as I'm finished talking to him."

"Great. You want to know if he gets worried, or if he calls someone as soon as you leave, that sort of thing?" she asked, her excitement showing in her voice.

"Right. If I can make him nervous, we'll know that he has something to hide."

"But what?" she asked.

"That I don't know. That may be the hard part, figuring out what he has to do with any of this, if anything."

"When do we go?"

"Right now."

It was good to see her enthusiasm, yet at the same time I was worried about Monica's safety. I had seen this sort of reaction from young rookie police officers. I had seen the results, too. Too many times in the course of their own excitement, they had made mistakes that had cost them their lives or the life of their partner.

But on the other hand, I could not think of anyone that I would rather have for a partner. She was smart, careful, and she had that special instinct that some officers never develop, the ability to say just the right thing at just the right time.

"I'm ready," she announced with a big grin.

"No, you're not. I need you to look like someone who has money to spend when you enter that store. You need to look like a million bucks, not that you don't already."

"Thank you."

Monica smiled a devilish smile. I knew she had something in mind when she turned and left for the bedroom. I wondered what it was. It was not long before I found out. Within a few minutes, she came out of the bedroom wearing a summer dress that made her look like a million bucks.

"How's this?" she asked as she turned around so I could see the skirt fan out in a circle.

"That's great. Perfect."

"What would you think if I took the pin with the family crest on it and asked him to appraise it for me? It would give me a good reason to be in the store."

"That's a good idea. It might prove to be very interesting, too. However, it could also prove to be dangerous as well. If he knows who the pin belongs to, you could be in a lot of danger."

"True, but you'd be right there to protect me."

"Okay," I agreed reluctantly.

I had to admit that it was a good idea to have some valid reason for her to be in the store, and it might prove interesting if Fox knew something about the pin. It could be the one thing that might lead us to who had given the pin to Robin.

After I retrieved the pin from under the chair, we went down to the garage and got in my car. We drove downtown to the jewelry store where we hoped to find Travis Fox working.

The store was located near the corner of East State and Broadway only a few blocks from the Performing Arts Center. I found a place nearby to park the car.

After parking the car, I sat for a minute looking out the front windshield. I was still worried that something might go wrong with our plan. It didn't seem right having a civilian in on this, even if it was Monica. Yet, there was no one that I trusted more.

"Ready?" she asked as if she knew what I was thinking.

I turned and looked at her. I wasn't sure if I was ready or not, or if this was still a good idea, but Monica was ready and that seemed to be enough for me.

"Yeah. Give me about five minutes before you come in."

"Okay," she replied as she forced a thin smile.

From the look on Monica's face I could tell that she was nervous. I thought seriously of calling the whole thing off and confronting Fox alone.

"You don't have to do this if you don't want to."

"I want to do it," she said with a sigh. "I'm ready."

I leaned over and gave her a light kiss on the lips and a wink before I got out of the car. Walking around the corner, I took a second to stop and turn around to look back at Monica. She had been watching me and gave me a wink and a smile. I was sure that it was her way of letting me know that she was ready before I disappeared around the corner.

A small bell over the door rang as I walked into the store. I took a minute to look around. The store had all the typical glass cases found in most jewelry stores. However, the back wall seemed bare of any kind of decorations. The back wall was almost completely covered with mirrors. I had to wonder if the wall was made up of one-way mirrors that would allow anyone in the back of the store to see out to the showroom floor.

There was a little old man sitting in a corner at a large desk and worktable. He was neatly dressed, wearing a white shirt and tie, and dark blue trousers. He had an eyepiece attached to his wire rimmed glasses. My guess was that he was the one who would be able to tell the value of a gem or fix your expensive watch. Fox was probably just a salesman.

Behind one of the counters was a rather tall man with dark wavy hair and a pleasant smile for the customer he was waiting on. He was wearing a very well tailored gray suit that gave him the appearance of someone who was proud of his appearance. He also gave a person the feeling that he knew his business well. His appearance instilled a certain amount of confidence in his judgment. He seemed perfect for this business.

I waited the couple of minutes that it took for him to finish with the woman he had been waiting on. When he was finished, I walked up to the counter and looked down into the glass case at some rather expensive rings.

"May I help you, sir?" His voice and demeanor was very pleasant.

"I would like to speak with Mr. Travis Fox, please."

"I'm Travis Fox. What can I help you with?"

I reached inside my jacket pocket and pulled out my badge and ID.

"I'm Detective McCord of the Milwaukee Police Department."

The appearance of my badge and my introduction caused the pleasant smile to quickly fade away into a stern, cold look. His eyes narrowed. I could see an instant dislike for me.

"I'm investigating the murder of Miss Robin Flower. I'd like to ask you a couple of questions if I may?"

"You may not," he replied harshly.

"Well, Mr. Fox, we can do this the easy way or the hard way. If you don't wish to answer a few questions for me now, I will arrest you and take you downtown for questioning. I don't want to have to take you away from your work just to ask you a few simple questions, but I will. Are you going to force me to take you downtown?" I asked, looking him straight in the eye.

"What do you want to know?" he asked reluctantly.

"You were at the South Shore Park on the day that Miss Flower's body was found."

"You already know that or you wouldn't be here," he interrupted.

"That's true. What I would like to know is what were you doing in the park that day?"

He looked into my eyes for several moments. I began to wonder if he was going to answer me.

"I got a phone call from someone I know. He asked me to meet him in the park."

"Did he show up?"

"As a matter of fact, no, he didn't."

"Why not?"

"I don't think that's any of your business."

The tone of his voice was growing sharper with each answer. It was clear that I was going to get very little out of him, but I had to try.

"Would you mind telling me who it was that you were to meet?"

"Yes, yes I would mind. Now I have a customer," he said as he turned and walked toward the other end of the counter.

I glanced over to see Monica walking up to the end of the counter. I stood there for several seconds as I watched him move down the counter to where Monica stood before I turned and walked out the door.

Once outside, I walked down the sidewalk until I was just past the windows. I turned and stood at the edge of one of the windows where I could see what was going on in the store.

I watched as Monica handed him the pin with the family crest on it. He looked several times from the pin to Monica and back to the pin again. The expression on his face gave me the feeling that he recognized the pin, or at least knew something about it.

Their conversation went on for several minutes as he nervously turned the pin over and over in his hand. I was hoping that Monica wasn't getting in too deep. The longer she was in the store with Fox, the more concerned I became about her.

I let out a sigh of relief when I saw Fox give the pin back to Monica. The look on Fox's face and the manner in which he gave it to her made me think that there was something about the pin that was special to him. I noticed Monica say something to him, then she turned and walked out the door.

I waited at the window while Monica walked by me to make sure that Fox was not going to follow her. He did watch her very closely as she left, but that didn't bother me as much as the look on his face. If he had looked at her as if she were a beautiful woman, which she is, I could understand that. But the look on his face was more like that of a man who had seen a ghost, or something that caused him a great deal of concern. It was clear that the pin had disturbed Fox very much and I wondered why. What did he know about the pin?

Fox suddenly looked around the store as if to see if he was being watched. He seemed nervous, almost frightened. He quickly turned and went through a door to the back of the store.

I quickly turned and caught up with Monica at the car. I motioned for her to get in. I immediately started the car and pulled way from the curb.

"Get down," I instructed her as I drove around the corner.

"What's happened?" she asked as she scooted down.

"Fox went into the back of the store as soon as you left. I want to see if he is going out the back through the alley."

As I came up to the alley, I slowed down and stopped. I looked down the alley toward the back of the store. The alley was empty except for the usual dumpsters and junk left in such places. Fox had gone to the back of the store, but he had not come out the back, as least as far as I could tell.

After waiting for several minutes, I started up again and drove on down the street. Monica sat up in the seat and looked at me.

"Did you see the look on his face when I showed him the pin?" she asked excitedly.

"Yes."

"I wonder what it was that made him so nervous. He almost jumped out of his skin."

"I don't know, but one thing is for sure. He recognized that pin. The fact that you had it rattled his cage. It will be interesting to find out what Sam can tell us about it."

"He should have the pictures of it by late this afternoon. We can call him in the morning and see what he has to say about it. What do we do now?"

"I'm taking you back to my apartment. After that, I'm going to visit Mr. Joe Martonie."

"Who is he?"

"He is one of Frank Angelini's enforcers and body-guards. He was at the park when Robin's body was found."

"Can I go with you?"

"Not this time."

Monica sat back against the seat and looked straightforward out the window. I knew that she wanted to go along, but this visit was going to take me to Angelini's house, and I did not want her there.

As soon as we arrived at my apartment, we sat down and discussed what transpired between Monica and Fox in the jewelry store.

"He asked me where I got such a pin," Monica explained.

"What did you tell him?"

"I told him I found it among some things that I inherited from my mother. That seemed to surprise him. He just stared at the pin for several seconds before he said anything more."

"Do you think he believed you?"

"I think so, but I can't be sure. Do you know that he has a little twitch under his left eye when he gets nervous?" she asked with a grin. "I don't even think he realizes he does it."

"Did he ask you anything else about the pin?"

"No. It was strange, but he seemed to be more interested in my background. He asked me a lot of questions. Where my mother was from? Was I of Italian ancestry? What part of Italy was my family from? What was my grandmother's maiden name?"

"What did you tell him?"

"I told him that I thought my grandmother was from Southern Italy, but that my mother had been born in New York. And I told him that I wasn't sure what my grandmother's maiden name was."

"Good. That should keep him thinking for a while. You did very well."

"Since I did so well, can I go with you to question Martonie?" she asked using her sweet soft voice.

"No. Not this time. You did a great job with Fox, but that was in a public place where he was far less likely to do something stupid. My visit with Martonie will be at Frank Angelini's home, not so public," I replied.

"Oh. Be careful," she said, the tone of her voice showing that she was concerned.

"I will."

It was getting on towards mid-afternoon and I needed to question Martonie. I gave Monica a light kiss and told her that I would be back before dinner, then left for my visit with Joe Martonie.

Angelini's place was out in one of the more affluent neighborhoods of Milwaukee. It would take me about forty-five minutes to get there which would give me time to think about Martonie's possible involvement in Robin's death.

CHAPTER TEN

I drove down the tree-lined street toward Angelini's home. The houses in this area of town were very large and nestled in among large old trees behind tall brick and concrete walls. Most of the homes had big decorative iron gates at the entrances with state of the art security systems, and a few of them had security guards. Several of the houses reminded me of old English fortresses, only lacking a guard at the front gate wearing the bright red coat and tall bear fur hat.

The Angelini estate was surrounded by a thick wall with iron spikes sticking out of the top. The wall was about eight feet high. As I turned in the drive, I was instantly greeted by a tall and very heavy iron gate. Next to the gate was a guardhouse with a uniformed security guard inside. A quick look around revealed two security cameras, one on top of the wall and one close to the gate pointed directly at me.

"This place is guarded better than Fort Knox," I said to myself as I pulled up and stopped next to the guardhouse.

The security guard sat in the guardhouse for a minute looking over my dark green Dodge. I was sure that he was thinking that I should go around to the service entrance and not come through the front gate. He finally got up, came out of the guardhouse and leaned over to look at me.

"I'm Detective McCord with the Milwaukee Police Department. I would like to speak with Joe Martonie," I said as I held up my ID and badge for the security guard to see.

"Do you have an appointment to see him?"

"No," I replied thinking that I was not about to let this rent-a-cop prevent me from seeing Martonie.

"I'm sorry, but I cannot let you in without an appointment."

"I'm going to say this just once, so you better listen very carefully. You get on your little phone in there and call up to the house. You tell whoever answers the phone, to get Martonie down here before I have half of the Milwaukee Police Department camped right here on Frank Angelini's front door step until Martonie comes out to talk to me. You got that?"

"Yes, sir."

I watched as the security guard slowly backed away from my car and turned around to go into the guardhouse. He picked up the phone and made a call. The expression on his face as he tried to explain the situation to someone on the other end might have been funny if my reason for being here had been different. I noticed the security guard nodded a few times. I could see him mouth the words "Yes, sir" a couple of time before he hung up the phone.

As he came out of the guardhouse, I had to wonder at the expression on his face what he was going to say. I couldn't tell if he was going to let me in or not, but I got the impression that he didn't like what he had been told. I sat in my car and waited for him to come to me.

"You are to drive up to the front of the main house where you will be met by Mr. Angelini and Mr. Martonie," he said calmly and without any emotion at all.

I nodded that I understood and waited for him to return to the guardhouse to open the gates. The large iron gates slowly opened and I drove through.

The driveway to the house was long and lined with clusters of different colored rose bushes in full bloom. The lawn was neatly cut and trimmed making it look like a dark green carpet. The house was a three-story stucco house with a long porch running across the front. The large columns gave it an almost roman style. The driveway curved around with a wide area in front of the house for parking.

I immediately noticed a man standing on the front porch looking in my direction. It had to be Joe Martonie, but at this distance I was not completely sure. As I got closer I could see that it was Martonie. He stood about six-one with the build of an athlete. He was an intimidating figure standing there with his arms crossed in front of him without a hint of a smile.

As I pulled up in front of the house, the front door opened and Frank Angelini stepped out onto the porch next to Martonie. They didn't move, they simply watched and waited for me to get out of my car and come up onto the porch to them.

"Afternoon, Frank," I said as I stepped up onto the porch.

"What do you want, McCord?" Frank said sharply.

"I want to have a little talk with Martonie, if you don't mind."

"I do mind. Joe works for me."

"I know that, but I don't care who he works for. I still want to have a talk with him. I can talk to him here, in private, or I can have him brought downtown and talk to him there. Which is it going to be?"

"I don't mind talking to him, Mr. Angelini. I know McCord from a few years back," Martonie said sort of quietly.

"You don't have to talk to him without an attorney, Joe."

"You want an attorney, Martonie?" I asked as I watched his face for some kind of clue as to what was going on in his head.

"I don't need no attorney to talk to you, unless you plan to arrest me for somethin', cause I didn't do nothin'."

"I just want to ask you a few questions about the day you were in the park when Robin Flower's body was found."

Joe looked at me as if he wasn't sure if I was telling the truth. I was hoping that we could talk alone, but at the moment I had my doubts that Frank would allow that.

"It's okay Mr. Angelini. I'll talk to him. I got nothin' to hide."

"You call me if he gets pushy, you understand?" Frank advised him. "He has no right to be here without a warrant."

"I understand, Mr. Angelini," Joe said.

"If it will ease your concerns, Frank, I don't think Joe had anything to do with the murder of Robin Flower."

Frank looked at Joe, then at me. It was apparent that he was concerned about Joe, but he relented and went back into the house leaving us along on the porch.

Joe motioned for me to follow him to the end of the porch. Near the end of the porch were a couple of chairs, and Joe gestured for me to sit down. As I sat down, he sat down in a chair facing me.

"Well, what do you want to know?" he asked as if he wanted me to get right to the point.

"Why were you in the park the day Robin was found dead?"

"I was there to see someone."

"Who?"

"I don't know."

"You were there to see someone, but you don't know who? Doesn't that sound a little lame to you? It certainly does to me."

"I guess it does, but that's why I was there."

"Let's back up a little. Someone wanted to meet with you in the park and you agreed to meet them, but you don't know who it was you were to meet, right?"

"Right," he replied seeming to be glad that I understood.

"Okay. Why don't you explain this to me?"

"I got a phone call the day Miss Flower was found dead. You can ask Mr. Angelini, he was there when I got the call.

"Anyway, I got this call and the person said that I should meet him in South Shore Park near the kiddies' swings at about two o'clock. He said not to tell anybody, including Mr. Angelini, where I was going, but to be there. He said to be sure to come alone, that he had important information that he knew my boss, Mr. Angelini, would want to know."

"Didn't it seem a little strange to you that he had information that Frank would want to know, yet he told you not to tell Frank that you were going to meet him?"

It was rapidly becoming apparent that Martonie was not very sharp. Frank had found a man who was loyal and strong like a big dog, but lacked the ability to think for himself. I had to question if Martonie had the capacity to murder the girl, especially in the way she was killed.

"I guess you're right. I hadn't thought about it. I just did what he asked."

"You like Frank, don't you?"

"I sure do. He's a good man. He gave me a job when I needed one. He helped put my younger sister through college, and he looks out for me."

"You'd do anything for Frank wouldn't you?"

"Yeah, I guess I would. Except for murder," he added after a short hesitation. "I wouldn't do that for no one."

"How did you feel about young Mr. Angelini's girl friend, Robin?"

"She was nice. I'll miss seeing her around here. She was always nice to me. She'd talk to me when none of the others would."

"What about young Mr. Angelini, Tony, do you like him?" I asked as I watched his eyes.

Joe hesitated to answer for a few seconds. He looked like he was trying to figure out how to avoid answering my question without making it sound like he didn't like Tony.

"He's all right, I guess," he finally replied.

"What do you mean by that? Didn't the two of you get along?"

"We got along, most of the time. He'd – ah - he didn't like me talking to Miss Flower."

"Why?"

"I don't know. I guess cause he didn't like no one talking to her."

I didn't know Tony very well. Most of my dealings with the Angelini family had been with his father, Frank, or with Frank's enforcers. The fact that Tony Angelini was the jealous type came as news to me, although I wasn't overly surprised. The only question now was, just how jealous a man was Tony? Jealous enough to have Robin killed? Jealous enough to kill her in an angry rage?

"Joe, you've been a big help. There's just one other question that I would like to ask. Are you related to Frank?"

"Yes, I guess."

"Don't you know?"

"No, not really. I was married to Frank's younger sister. She died of cancer last year after being sick for a long time," he said softly.

I was sure that I saw a small tear come to his eye. It was clear that Joe had loved his wife and missed her now that she was gone. I was sure that Joe had nothing else to do, so he stayed on with Frank.

"I'm sorry to hear about your loss, Joe."

"Thanks," he replied.

"Thanks for your help. I'll see you around," I said as I stood up.

"That's all you wanted?"

The look on his face and his question was almost funny. I guess that he had expected me to drill him like I did when I arrested him for running over an old man several years ago.

"Yeah. That's all."

I turned and walked along the porch toward the steps. As I turned to go down the steps to my car, Frank came out of the house onto the porch. He looked over at Joe, then back at me.

"You finished already?"

"I am for now."

"You're not going to arrest Joe on some trumped-up change?" Frank asked sarcastically.

"I have no reason to arrest Joe, at this time."

"You're not going to help me find out who killed my son's fiancée, are you?"

"You got that right, Frank. I'm going to find out who did it, and why. Then I'm going to see to it that they pay, legal like."

"Your courts will not do justice to whoever it was," Frank said angrily.

"And yours will?"

"You can bet on it, McCord."

"Right," I replied sarcastically, then turned my back on Frank and walked down the steps to my car.

Just before getting into my car, I glanced up and saw Joe walk up next to Frank. Frank was standing at the edge of the porch watching me.

I got into my car and drove down the driveway to the gate. As I approached the gate, it started to open. I drove through the gate out onto the street and pointed my car toward downtown.

As I drove, I mentally sorted through my list of suspects. Other than Lieutenant Brooks, there was only one who I had not questioned yet. Charley Mitken. I can't say for sure, but I had to wonder if I had subconsciously put off questioning Charley because he was the meanest one of the bunch. Now it was time to talk to him.

I drove to the neighborhood where Mitken was supposed to live. It was certainly not the classiest part of town. The streets were lined with rundown bars, pool halls, cheap hotels, and prostitutes. The latest address I had on Mitken was in a cheap hotel above the Silver Cue Pool Hall.

It didn't take me long to find the hotel. The entrance was sandwiched in between a liquor store and the Silver Cue. I parked my car in front and got out. I took a few minutes to look around before I pushed open the door and entered the hotel.

As I entered, I noticed that the lobby was dingy and dirty. The walls looked as if they had not been washed in fifty years. The paint was pealing off the ceiling, and the ceiling fan was caked with years of dust and dirt, and it smelled of stale cigarettes. In a corner sat an old man with eyes that appeared tired and sad. He watched me as I walked past him to the desk. I stepped up to the desk and rang the little bell.

"Yeah. What'd you want?" an unshaven, dirty man with a black cigar in his mouth asked.

"What room is Charley Mitken in?"

"Who wants to know?"

"I do," I said with a demanding tone in my voice as I held my badge and ID out where he could see it.

"Second floor, third door on the right," he answered instantly when he saw my badge.

He quickly looked away as if he was afraid I might recognize him. He sat back down and went back to watching the old television. As a matter of fact, I did recognize him. I had arrested him awhile back for some petty offense that I couldn't even remember.

I turned and looked up the stairs, but hesitated for a moment. I turned back toward the desk and looked at the clerk.

"Stay off that phone if you know what's good for you."

He glanced in my direction, nodded that he understood. I turned and started up the stairs. The stairs creaked and squeaked under my weight as I climbed them. Once in the hall, I found it dingy and dark like the lobby. What few lights remained in the fixtures did little to light the hall.

When I got to the third door on the right, I stopped and carefully listened at the door. I couldn't hear any noise coming from inside the room. I drew my 9mm pistol from under my coat and stepped to one side of the door.

Just as I was ready to knock on the door and identify myself, I was startled by the door across the hall opening. I swung around and pointed my gun toward the door. An old man stepped out into the hall. He stopped in his tracks at the sight of my gun.

"Get back in your room," I instructed him.

"If you're looking for Charley, he ain't in. He's in the Silver Cue playin' pool," the man said, his eyes showing how nervous he was at the sight of the gun in my hand.

"Are you sure?"

"Yeah. He's been there for the past two hours. I just left him there. He's wearin' blue pants, a black shirt with the sleeves rolled up and a yellow tie."

"You stay here," I said as I put my gun back under my coat and went back down the hall.

I went through the lobby and out onto the sidewalk. Turning right, I went into the Silver Cue. After stepping into the poolroom, I stepped to one side of the door to allow my eyes to adjust to the dimly lit, smoke filled room. Within seconds, I spotted Charley. He had his back to me and had not seen me come in. He was leaning over the pool table taking aim on the blue ball in front of the corner pocket. I moved up closer to him, and waited for him to make his shot.

Slipping my hand under my coat, I wrapped my fingers around my pistol before I spoke.

"Nice shot, Charley."

Charley straightened up and spun around to face me. He stared at me with narrowed eyes filled with hatred. He didn't seem at all surprised to see me. It was as if he had been waiting for me to show up.

I noticed that he carefully and cautiously changed his grip on the cue stick he had clutched in his hands. There was no doubt in my mind that he was going to try to use it on me. There was also no doubt in my mind that I was going to prevent him from doing so.

"Don't do anything that you will regret, Charley. I just want to talk to you," I said slowly and clearly so that there was no mistake as to what I meant.

"I'll talk to you, all right."

Charley's voice was harsh and threatening as he gripped the cue stick in both hands and took a step toward me. In one smooth, flowing motion, I pulled my gun out from under my coat and stuck it right in his face. The barrel was only a few inches from the end of his nose.

He stopped suddenly, not making another move as he stared into the barrel. There was no longer the look of hatred in his eyes, only fear.

Slowly, the focus of his eyes moved from the gun barrel to my face. I could see that his mind was turning over and over the question of whether or not I would pull the trigger.

"Put the cue stick down real slow," I said calmly. "I just want to talk."

I watched his eyes, and he watched mine. It was a war of nerves. Who would be the first to give in and let his guard down?

Slowly, Charley straightened to his full height of six-one. He hesitated, but finally reached back and laid the cue stick down on the pool table. I kept my gun pointed in his face until he let go of the cue stick and put his hands down at his sides.

"Okay, I put it down," he said again looking down the barrel.

Without taking my eyes off him, I slowly lowered my gun as I stepped back a little. It was not wise to trust him completely, so I decided to keep the gun in my hand.

Charley was not the smartest person in the world, and he just couldn't wait to get to me. As soon as my gun was pointed toward the floor, he lunged at me. I quickly stepped aside causing him to go right past me. As he went by, I hit him hard at the base of the neck between the shoulder blades with my gun. The sudden shock to the upper spine caused him to go crashing to the floor with little or no feeling in his legs. I knew it would not last long, but it would last long enough for him to think twice before he tried something that stupid again.

I sat down in a chair next to him. He slowly rolled over and looked up at me from the floor. I still had my gun pointed at him.

"You don't listen very well, do you? I'm going to ask you a few questions. If I get reasonably good answers, I'll leave. If I don't, I'll cuff and stuff you, and throw you in jail until I get what I want."

"You can't do that," he said, his voice showing that he was in some pain from the hit to his upper spine.

"I not only can, but I will. You're a two time loser. One more and you'll be an old man before you get out of the joint. Now are you going to cooperate with me?"

I sat back in the chair while I gave Charley a moment or two to think over what I had said. I didn't take my gun off him, however.

"Can I get up?" he asked after he took a few moments to think about what I said.

"I don't think so. You've already demonstrated that you can't be trusted. You stay right there until we're done.

"You were at South Shore Park when Robin Flower's body was found. What were you doing in the park?"

"I was there to meet someone."

"That seems to be the stock answer these days."

"What do you mean by that?"

"Nothing. Who were you supposed to meet?"

"That's none of your business," he blurted out.

"Now, I thought we had sort of an understanding here. You answer my questions and I don't get mad and make things really tough on you. Who were you there to meet?"

"I was there to meet Danny Minger," he replied more softly.

"Danny Minger! Why Danny?"

"Cause that's who I was told to meet. I was told to meet him in the park near the kiddies' sand box."

"Who told you to meet Danny there?"

"I can't.... I don't know. I got a phone call here. I was told to meet Danny, that's all."

"You're not going to tell me who called you, are you?"

"I'll be dead before dark if I do," he replied making it very clear that I was not going to get it out of him.

"Like Danny?"

"What?"

"Danny is already dead."

Charley closed his eyes as if he suddenly realized that his life was not worth a nickel even if he didn't talk. I was hoping that he would decide to talk to me. When he opened his eyes and looked up at me, I knew that he had said all he was going to say. I could see no reason to continue this conversation.

"I'm going to leave now. Stay face down on the floor until I'm gone," I instructed him as I stood up.

With my gun still pointed at him, he did as he was told. I backed toward the door. When I reached the door, I put my gun back under my coat and stepped out onto the sidewalk. I got in my car and drove off.

As I drove toward my apartment, I reviewed the answers that I had been getting from those I had questioned. In every case, all my suspects were told by someone to go to the park on that date, at that time. Who wanted them all in the park at the same time, but more importantly, why?

Danny had said that he thought it was Travis Fox who had contacted him to go to the park to make a sale, but who was it that got Travis Fox, Charley Mitken, Robert Goouchie and Joe Martonie in the park all at the same time?

CHAPTER ELEVEN

I pulled into the parking lot of my apartment a little before dinnertime. After driving into the garage, I sat in the car staring out the windshield, but I was not looking at the wall in front of me. I was busy thinking.

This case was getting a little too complex to suit me. I had too many suspects for this type of murder, and one of my suspects was already dead. I found it strange that all of the suspects had been in the same place, at the same time, and for the same reason. They had all been telephoned and instructed to be in the park at approximately two in the afternoon. In order to get all of them in the park at the same time, there had to be one common denominator. There had to be that one person who knew all of them well enough to get them to do as he asked.

The one thing that kept coming back to mind over and over again was the idea that Lieutenant Brooks had something to do with all this, but what? What was his part in this? Who was he working for? How deeply was he involved?"

I thought about asking Captain Sinclair to question Brooks, but it was still a little premature. Besides, I still hadn't displaced all my thoughts that Captain Sinclair might have a hand in this in some way.

It was time for me to get something to eat and sleep on it for a little while. Some rest and time to think was what I needed in the hope of getting a fresh outlook on it.

I got out of the car and went up to my apartment. The thought that Monica would be there made the three flights of stairs a lot easier to climb.

When I got to the top of the stairs and turned onto the landing, I glanced toward my apartment door. I stopped suddenly. A cold chill passed through me like an ice cube sliding down my back. The door to the apartment was open. It was only slightly ajar, but that was enough to not only alert me, but to frighten me as well. I froze in my tracks.

The first thing that came to mind was Angelini. I had to wonder if Angelini might have found out that I had the broach. The other thought that came to mind was he had decided that since I wasn't telling him what he wanted to know, he was looking for a way to force me to tell him.

My mind quickly filled with questions. Was Monica all right? Was she hurt? Had she been taken, kidnapped? The thought that one of Angelini's hoods might still be in the apartment with her caused me to make urgent, rapid decisions.

The one thing that I quickly realized was that I could not be any help to Monica if I didn't control my own thoughts. I reached under my jacket and wrapped my fingers around the grip of my gun. Drawing it out, I moved silently up close to the wall. Leaning against the wall next to the door I listened for any kind of noise, but I heard nothing.

I reached over and slowly pushed the door open wider, but I could still not see anything. I stepped into the room with my gun at the ready, afraid of what I might find.

Suddenly, the door from my bedroom opened. I quickly swung around and pointed my gun in that direction. Monica let out a scream at the sight of my gun pointed at her, and I quickly jerked it away.

"What are you doing?" she screamed at me, her eyes as big as saucers and her voice catching as she gasped for air.

"Are you all right?"

"I'm fine. At least I was until I saw that cannon of yours pointed at me," she said as she tried to regain her breath.

"I'm sorry. I didn't mean to scare you, but you scared the hell out of me. The door was open. What was I supposed to think?"

"I saw you drive in the garage. I just opened the door for you," she explained.

Now I did feel like a fool.

"Don't ever leave the door open like that. I was sure that someone had broken in. I don't even want to think about what went through my mind, and of all things that might have happened to you."

"What took you so long to get up here?"

"I was thinking. This case has got me baffled."

"What you need is a good meal and a good night's rest. You're working too hard. Dinner will be ready in a few minutes. Why don't you sit down and relax for a few minutes. And put that gun away."

"I think I will, if you don't mind."

Monica stepped up to me and gave me a quick kiss on the cheek, then went out to the kitchen. As I watched her walk away, I couldn't help but wonder what she saw in me. We are from completely different worlds, yet we seem to be made for each other.

After putting my gun away in the closet, I sat down in my Lazy Boy recliner and tipped back. It had been an interesting day, but there was one thing that seemed to stick in my mind. Although each of my suspects had been summoned to the park, two were afraid for their lives if someone found out who had sent them to the park. One of them was already dead, the other I left lying on the floor in a poolroom.

The thought passed through my head that Charley Mitken might try to run to avoid the same fate as Danny Minger. I considered having an APB put out for his arrest, but I had done that with Danny. I found out the hard way that I was unable to protect him, even in jail. I hated to admit it, but maybe he did have a better chance of surviving if he ran.

My thoughts were interrupted when Monica called me to dinner. I got up and went out to the kitchen.

"Were you able to talk to Joe Martonie?" Monica asked as we sat down at the table.

"Yes. Joe is not all that bad a guy, a little misguided, maybe. I also think he's a little slow upstairs, but something tells me that he couldn't have killed Robin. From the look in his eyes when he talked about her, I don't think he had anything to do with it. I get the feeling that he really liked her, possibly even loved her from a distance."

"Where does that leave you?"

"Just about where I started. I don't seem to be getting any closer to solving this case."

"What about this - - - Charley - - - what's his name?"

"Charley Mitken. I don't know about him."

"Have you talked to him?" Monica asked as she took a fork full of salad.

"I talked to him, but he wasn't talking very much. I get the feeling that he knows more than he's telling me. In fact, I'm sure of it. He got kind of scared when I tried to get him to tell me who it was that told him to meet Danny Minger in the park."

"He was supposed to meet Danny Minger in the park?" Monica asked with surprise.

"That's what he said. Why?"

"I thought you told me Danny was afraid of Charley."

"I did," I said as I remembered that Danny had told me that Charley hated him.

"What would make Charley go to the park to meet someone he hated?" Monica asked as she looked across the table at me.

"I don't know, but it had to be important," I said thoughtfully.

"It must have been very important to Charley because he went. Maybe he owed someone a favor, or someone was paying him to meet Danny," Monica added.

"There's nothing in his file that would indicate that he works for anyone except himself. If he was being paid, I'm sure he was paid a lot. If he owed someone a favor, it had to be someone who had something really big to hold over his head."

"Possibly Frank Angelini?"

"Maybe, but I don't think so. Frank wouldn't want to be associated with the likes of Charley. He's been arrested too many times and is too hard to control. Frank likes to keep a low profile. He would use one of his own men or get someone from out of town before he would use someone like Charley."

"Have you thought that you might be looking too far from the source?"

"What do you mean?"

"Well, it's a long shot, but maybe it's the younger Angelini you should be talking to," Monica suggested.

I thought about what she said for a minute. I didn't know Tony very well. I hadn't had any dealings with him.

"You might be right. When I talked to Joe Martonie, he said Tony was jealous of anyone who even talked to Robin."

"Is it possible that Tony killed Robin because he found out that she was seeing someone else or thought that she was seeing someone else?" Monica asked.

"It's possible, I guess, but this was not your ordinary killing. She was given an overdose of cocaine, then shot in the head execution style after she was already dead. That's not the normal way of getting rid of someone because of jealousy. In a fit of rage, you don't kill a person twice," I said.

Monica sat there and looked at me while I thought about what she had said. Slowly, it came to me what she was getting at. The shot in the back of the head was probably a clumsy attempt to cover up the death by cocaine. Since anyone with any brains at all would know that an autopsy would be done and evidence of the cocaine would be found. Maybe it was more of an attempt to make things difficult to prove.

Just then the ringing of my phone interrupted my thoughts. I got up from the table, went into the living room and picked up the receiver.

"Hello."

"Nick, this is Jerry."

"What's up?"

"Remember that letter you told me about that was hidden in the stove?"

"Sure, what about it?"

"It was a note from Robin Flower."

"To her mother," I said.

"No. To Mr. Angelini."

"What?"

"Yeah. Inside the envelope addressed to Rose Flower was another envelope addressed and ready to mail to Mr. Angelini."

"Which Mr. Angelini?"

"The old man, Frank."

"You're kidding?"

"No. It was addressed to Frank Angelini."

Needless to say I was a little surprised. I looked toward the kitchen and saw Monica standing in the doorway. She must have seen the look on my face as she straightened up and walked across the room to me. She sat down on the sofa and leaned over, putting her ear next to the phone.

"What did the note say?"

Jerry began reading the letter to me.

"Dear Mr. Angelini. I know how much you love Tony, so do I. But even as much as I love him, I can not marry someone who uses drugs. I'm sorry to inform you that Tony

has been using drugs on a regular basis for several years. I just found out, myself. I'm sure you would want to know so that you could help him get off them. I have asked him not to use them, but he still does. I'm sorry to have to tell you this, as I know it will hurt you deeply. I didn't want to do that. I hope that you can help him, as we both love him. Love Robin."

"Does anyone else know about this letter?"

"No. I didn't let Bob Wray know that I had it."

"Keep it to yourself. I don't want anyone to know about it, not even Captain Sinclair. You hide it where no one will find it."

"Okay."

"Are you sure Robin wrote the letter?"

"Reasonably sure. The only fingerprints on the letter belong to Robin."

"Great. Do you..."

"I hear someone coming, got to go," Jerry said, interrupting me.

The next sound I heard was that of the phone going dead. I hung up the receiver and looked at Monica.

"Your theory just might be right."

"What theory?"

"The one that says I should be looking at Tony, not Frank, but not because of jealousy," I said.

"Then what?" Monica asked, the expression on her face indicating that she didn't understand what I was getting at.

"If Tony found out that Robin was going to tell his father that he was using drugs, he might have come unglued and killed her. Frank may import and sell the stuff, but he would never allow any of his family to use it."

"Kind of a double standard, isn't it?" Monica commented.

"Oh yes. But more importantly, Frank would not want a charge of using drugs that close to the family. It causes too much suspicion. And you're right. Frank does hold a double standard. He expects his family to be above reproach, yet he is into drugs, extortion, and who knows what else."

"What's your next move?" Monica asked.

"I'm going to have a long talk with Jonathan Ehman and Tony Angelini. I think Ehman might be Tony's supplier. If not his supplier, he probably knows who is."

"Do you think it might be a little hard getting to Tony," Monica commented.

"I'll find a way. I'll start first thing in the morning with Ehman. I know where he lives. It would be my guess that he's a night person. The best time to catch him at home would be early in the morning while he's still in bed."

"But for the rest of tonight, you're mine," Monica said as she took hold of my hand.

"Oh, really?"

"Yes. You're going to spend a little time on me, and you're going to forget this case until morning."

"I am?" I asked, wondering what she had in mind.

"Yes. You are. I have to go back to Madison in a couple of days. I have no intention of spending all my time working on this case," she said as she leaned toward me.

I looked into those deep cobalt blue eyes as she reached out and put her soft hand on my face. Slowly, I leaned toward her until our lips met in a soft gentle kiss.

Gradually, our kiss became more passionate as her lips pressed against mine. Without thinking, I reached out and gently but firmly pulled her up against me. The feel of her body against me erased all thoughts of the case, at least for now. All I could think about was this beautiful woman who cared so much for me that she had dropped everything to come to me when I called.

I leaned back and looked into her eyes. They seemed to be full of love for me.

"It's almost time for the news. Why don't you watch it while I take a shower," Monica suggested.

I didn't say anything. I simply watched her as she got up and walked toward the bedroom. When she got to the bedroom door, she stopped and turned around to smile at me. She winked, then disappeared into the bedroom.

I sat there staring at the door she had gone through for several seconds. There was no doubt that this woman could get me to forget just about anything.

I glanced over at the television. My first thought was why would I want to watch television when there was such a beautiful and loving woman taking a shower in my bathroom. This was no time for me to be watching television. I got up and went into the bedroom. I could hear the shower running and walked over to the bathroom door. I gently knocked on the door.

"Yes?" I heard her reply.

"Would you like your back washed, lady?"

There was a short silence before her reply, "Is that all you want to wash?"

"Not if you would like me to wash more."

"There's not very much room in here," she called out playfully.

"I know."

"Then you better hurry before we run out of hot water."

I noted a slight giggle in her voice. As soon as I was undressed, I opened the door and walked into the bathroom. I could see her shapely figure silhouetted on the shower curtain. Pulling the curtain back, I stepped into the shower with her.

Monica immediately slid her hands up over my shoulders and around to the back of my head. Tipping her head up and to one side, she pressed her body to mine as our lips met in a warm passionate kiss.

The warm water cascaded over us as we held each other. I slid my hands up and down the smooth soft skin of her back. Her firm breasts pressed hard against my chest. A soft moan escaped her lips as my hands slid over her firm butt, pressing her flat stomach against me. At this moment, there was nothing else in the world, but us.

Leisurely, she loosened her hands from the back of my head. She leaned back, looked up and smiled at me. Her hair was flowing over her shoulders and there were droplets of water sparkling on her eyelashes.

"Wasn't the news interesting?" she asked playfully.

"Not as interesting as you," I replied as I gently squeezed her firm butt.

She reached behind me to the soap tray and picked up the soap. Holding it so I could see it, she asked. "You first?"

I smiled and took the bar of soap from her. She turned around and I began washing her smooth beautiful back.

We washed each other until the water began to get cold. After drying each other, I led her to my bed and pulled back the covers for her. We climbed into bed and wrapped ourselves in each other's arms.

Once again we spent the first part of the night escaping from the confusion of the day. Her body was soft and warm under my touch. We made love until we collapsed in each other's arms. We then drifted off to sleep, one of the most peaceful sleeps I could ever remember.

CHAPTER TWELVE

Morning came and I found myself lying on my side wrapped in Monica's arms. I could feel her warm breath on the back of my neck, and the warmth of her body lightly pressed against my back. My mind quickly remembered the love we had shared with each other before we drifted off to sleep. I felt comfortable lying in her arms, more comfortable than I felt I had a right to. I closed my eyes in the hope that this moment would not end, but this moment was to end.

As I lay there letting my mind wander, my thoughts turned to Robin Flower. Why had she been killed? Had she been killed simply because she was going to tell Tony's father that he was using drugs, or did she know something else that was far more dangerous? More importantly, who had taken that beautiful young woman's life?

My mind became so filled with thoughts of the case that I found I could not go back to sleep. I had things to do if I was going to find out who was responsible for Robin's death.

"What's the matter?" Monica asked as she squeezed me.

Monica had a way of knowing when I was worried, or when I had something that weighed heavily on my mind. I couldn't hide anything from her, not that I wanted to.

"I'm sorry, honey. I guess I've got a lot on my mind."

"I understand," she said softly. "I'll fix us breakfast before you go."

I couldn't help but feel her reluctance to let me go as she kissed me lightly on the back of the neck. I wanted to roll over and take her in my arms, but that would just delay what I had to do. It was better to get it out of the way and off my mind.

I sat up on the side of the bed and looked back over my shoulder. She looked so beautiful with her long blond hair fanned out around her face. I could only hope that she understood. Leaving her was the last thing I wanted to do, but I had work to do.

I got up and went into the bathroom. After I took a quick shower and shaved, I returned to the bedroom. Monica was gone. I dressed and put my gun in my belt holster. I hadn't thought about it for a very long time, but strapping on my gun was as much a part of dressing for me as putting on my shoes or my pants. For some reason I couldn't explain, that thought seemed to bother me this morning.

I went out to the kitchen and found Monica setting a plate of bacon and eggs on the table. She smiled, as she looked me over. Her eyes stopped when she saw my gun. The smile quickly faded from her face. At that moment I wished I had waited until I was ready to leave before putting it on.

"Are you all right?" I asked.

My question must have startled her. She quickly looked up at me. I could see the worry in her eyes.

"Please sit down. Your eggs will get cold," she said.

She sat down across the table from me. I was having a difficult time understanding her reaction this morning. It was almost as if she knew something was going to happen today, something that would prove to be very unpleasant.

I suddenly realized that she hadn't answered my question. Was she upset with me for having to leave her this morning? Was it my gun that caused her to worry or did it simply remind her of how dangerous the business I was in can be?

"Does it bother you that I carry a gun? If it does, I'll take it off until I leave."

"No, the gun doesn't bother me. I guess it reminds me of how much of a risk you take every day with some of the people that you have to deal with. I wouldn't want you to go out into the world without it."

I took a few bites of my breakfast. I wasn't sure how to reply to her or if a reply was really necessary. I had known so many women, mostly the wives of police officers, who hated the fact that their men had to carry guns. It would be impossible for me to imagine what it would be like if police officers didn't carry them.

"What are you going to do while I'm working?" I asked, not knowing what else to say.

"I thought I might go visit some of the sights, like the museums, maybe stop by the Performing Arts Center and see if there is something we might like to go see before I have to go back to Madison. Would you like to go to a play or a concert?"

"Sure. What time do you think you'll be back?"

"In time for lunch?" she asked, obviously wondering when I would like her back.

"There's a little cafe just around the corner from the Performing Arts Center. I could meet you in front of the center at noon and we could have lunch there. How's that sound?"

"That sounds great."

My suggestion to meet her for lunch seemed to raise her spirits. We finished our breakfast and she gave me a kiss before I left.

As I pulled out onto the street, I radioed in to let the Communications Center know that I was on duty, but didn't tell them where I was going. I headed straight to Ehman's address.

When I turned the corner onto the street where Ehman lived, I immediately noticed that it was a quiet street. The houses were close together and old, but generally in good condition. The neighborhood seemed to be a typical working class neighborhood with the usual three-to-four year old cars and a few pickup trucks parked in narrow driveways and on the street.

It didn't take me long to find the house where Ehman lived. It was a small brick house with a neat yard. The trim on the house needed painting, but the house looked homey.

I got out of my car and walked up the driveway to the front porch. I noticed that there was a six- or seven-year-old Chevy parked in the open garage, but no other vehicles around.

I stepped up on the porch, rang the doorbell and waited. I could hear the sound of footsteps as someone approached the door, followed by the sounds of a door being unlocked. The door opened just far enough for the woman to look out.

"Yes?"

"I'm Detective McCord of the Milwaukee Police Department," I said as I held out my badge and ID so the woman could see it. "I would like to know if Jonathan Ehman is home?"

It was clear by the expression on her face that the woman was not used to the police coming to her door. She looked confused and worried.

"Yes, he is. I'm his mother. What do you want to see him about?"

Her question was polite, yet demanding.

"I just want to talk to him for a few minutes."

"He works late down at one of the warehouses on the dock and he's still in bed. I don't want to disturb him."

"I'm sorry, ma'am, but I'm going to have to insist."

Reluctantly, she opened the door to let me in the house. As I stepped inside, she turned and started toward the back of the house. I assumed that she was going to wake her son.

"Please sit down," she said without turning around to speak to me directly.

I chose not to sit down, but rather moved a little further into the living room so that I could see down the hallway.

She stopped near the end of the hallway and knocked on a door. I could barely hear what she was saying.

"Jonathan - - - Jonathan."

She glanced back down the hallway and saw me standing in the living room watching her. She turned her back to me and leaned closer to the door. I couldn't hear what she was saying, but I was sure that she was telling him that I was here to talk to him.

The house was quiet this early in the morning, and the windows in the living room were open. Suddenly, I heard something fall outside the house, on the same side of the house as Jonathan's bedroom. My first thought was that he was going to try to escape out his bedroom window and run.

I turned and ran out the front door. As I turned the corner of the house, I saw Jonathan jump out the window onto the driveway. He looked over and saw me coming around the corner. He took off running toward the back of the house.

I took off up the driveway after him, jumping over the screen that had been pushed out of the window. He ran across the lawn and jumped a short fence, and I was right behind him. I followed him across a couple of other yards, over another fence and between a couple of houses. I ended up chasing him down the next street over.

I must have chased him about four blocks when I saw a police car stopped at corner. I pulled my badge out of my pocket and waved it at the patrolman in the car while still chasing Ehman. As soon as the patrolman noticed me, I pointed toward Ehman who was bit-by-bit leaving me behind. This kid could really run.

The patrolman in the car immediately turned on his lights and took off after Ehman. Ehman turned into an alley with the patrol car right on his heels. I lost sight of both of them until I got up to the alley. Looking down the alley, I saw the patrol car parked about half way down the block.

The door of the patrol car was standing open, but there was no patrol officer in sight.

Walking up to the patrol car, I stopped and looked around. There was no one around. I leaned against the patrol car and tried to catch my breath while I waited for the patrolman to return to his car. Needless to say, I was winded and needed the break.

I was beginning to think that I had lost Ehman and was going to have to put out an APB to find him. I didn't want to do that after what had happened to Danny, but it was beginning to look like Ehman was going to give me no choice.

My thoughts were disturbed when I heard a ruckus coming from down the alley. I turned around and saw the patrolman coming down the alley with Ehman. Although Ehman was putting up a fuss, he was no match for the officer. The officer had him by the scruff of the neck and was literally dragging him back to me.

"Where did you find him?" I asked the patrolman when I saw that Ehman looked like he had been dragged through the mud.

"I found him playing in a sprinkler in the back yard of a house around the corner," the patrolman answered with a wide grin.

I noticed that the patrolman didn't have a bit of dirt on him. My first thought was to ask the patrolman how he managed to catch Ehman without getting himself dirty or wet, but decided to forget it. My guess would be that he had pushed Ehman into the mud to stop him from running. Besides, it was not important how he caught him. I had Ehman and that was all I wanted.

"Thank you, I'll take him from here."

"He's all yours, Detective McCord."

I looked at the patrolman when he called me by name. Looking at the officer, I didn't recognize him. I must have looked a little confused.

"I met you at the police academy when you taught a class on preserving and gathering evidence at the scene of a crime."

"That was awhile ago. I haven't had time to teach for three or four years."

"Too bad. You were good at it."

"Thanks. And thanks for your help."

After this chase, I thought it might be a good idea if I cuffed Ehman. I had no desire to chase him again. If he decided to run again having his hands cuffed behind his back would certainly slow him down so I could at least catch him without help.

As soon as he was cuffed, the patrolman returned to his car and drove away. I began walking Ehman back to his house. I was sure that the neighbors were going to wonder why he was cuffed, but at this point I didn't care what the neighbors thought.

"Well Jonathan, was it worth it?"

"I almost got away," he said defiantly.

"Yeah, but you didn't. When are you going to learn that almost doesn't count? Where did you think you were going?"

"None of your business."

"But it is my business. You see, I know that you didn't find Miss Flower in the water. You found her on the beach at the edge of the water."

When I said that, he suddenly stopped and looked up at me. His eyes were big and I got the feeling that deep down he was scared to death. I had to wonder if he was scared for the same reason that Danny and Charley had been scared.

"You want to tell me what really happened on the beach."

"I told you already," his voice giving away the fact that he was not as sure of himself as he had been.

"Let's face it. I know what happened to her. What I don't know is what part you had in all this. It's time for you to start talking."

"My life won't be worth a nickel if I talk to you."

"Your life isn't worth that now. You know Danny Minger, don't you?"

"I've heard of him."

"You've more than heard of him. You bought drugs from him only hours before you found Robin."

"I don't use drugs," he said emphatically.

Now that was interesting. He says he doesn't use drugs, yet he bought drugs from Minger on several occasions, at least according to Minger.

"If you're not a user, then who are you buying for?"

"God, man. You really do want me dead, don't you?" he said.

The look on his face and the fear in his eyes was almost enough to convince me that he was in fear for his life. This young kid had gotten himself in way over his head. The only question was what had he gotten into?

"Tell you what. I'll give you some names and you tell me which one of them you were buying the drugs for, okay?"

Before he could answer my question, we had reached his house. His mother was standing on the porch with her hands over her mouth. The sight of her only son in cuffs must have been hard for her to take. I couldn't help but feel a little sorry for her.

"We can talk here or we can go downtown, which is it going to be?"

Ehman looked up at me, then at his mother. I could sense that he did not want his mother to know what he had been doing, but the thought of being taken downtown must have been even worse.

"Can we talk in my room?" he asked politely.

Now his voice indicated a willingness to cooperate. I removed the cuffs and we walked up the driveway to the porch. The confused look on his mother's face told me that she had no idea what her son had been doing.

"Jonathan, what's going on?" she asked as we stepped up on the porch.

"It's all right, mom. Detective McCord and I have to have a talk. I'll explain everything later."

She looked from her son to me, then back at her son as we entered the house. I followed Jonathan down the hall to his bedroom. He shut the door and sat down on the edge of the bed. I took the chair from in front of the small desk, set it down next to the door, and then sat down on it.

"Now, let's get down to business. Who were you buying drugs for?"

"I - - - I was buying them for Tony Angelini."

"Why?"

"Because he didn't want to get caught buying them."

"He deals in drugs, he could get all the drugs he wants. He certainly didn't need you to get them for him."

"Tony's father keeps real close records on everything. His father would know if he was taking any and would have a fit if he knew that his son was using drugs," Jonathan said.

"How did you get tied up with the Angelinis in the first place?"

"My mother doesn't know anything about this. Can we keep at least some of this from her?"

"I can't promise you anything."

"Yeah. I've heard about you," he said as he looked down at the floor.

"What have you heard about me?"

"You don't make any deals, and that you're a hard, by the book cop. You get onto something, you don't let go."

"What about you? Are you ready to talk, or are you going to keep up with the BS? How did you get involved with the Angelinis?"

He must have decided that it was over, that he had been caught and there was no way out for him. He must have realized that it was time to clear the slate and hope for the best. He lifted his face and looked at me as he began to tell his story.

"I work at a warehouse that is owned by the Angelini family. I stole some electrical equipment from the warehouse and sold it for the cash. I needed some money to help my mother. She thought I earned it at my job. During the investigation, Lieutenant Brooks figured out that I had taken the equipment."

So now I had my connection between Ehman and Brooks, but that still didn't help me much.

"Lieutenant Brooks didn't arrest me. I pleaded with him not to tell my mother because it would break her heart. My old man has hurt her enough. He up and left us. He's in jail in Illinois. You can check for yourself if you don't believe me.

"Lieutenant Brooks took me to an office in the warehouse where he questioned me. I didn't understand what he was getting at, at first, because a lot of his questions had nothing to do with what I had stolen. He didn't even seem to be interested in that at all.

"After a few hours, Tony Angelini shows up. I didn't know that Mr. Angelini owned the warehouse until then. I was sure that I was going to be fired and probably go to jail, and my mother would find out what I had done. Instead of firing me, Mr. Angelini said if I would do something for him, he would forget about what I had stolen."

"What did he ask you to do?"

"He asked me to find Danny Minger and buy drugs for him."

"Did you do it?"

"Hell yes, I did it. If I didn't he would've had me put in jail and my mother would find out everything and she would be alone. I couldn't have that happen."

"Let me fill in the rest," I suggested. "Tony continued to have you get drugs for him, using the threat of having you arrested and your mother finding out. Right?"

"Right."

"What about the girl? How did you get involved in that?"

"Lieutenant Brooks came to me at work just before I was to get off, it was a little before two in the morning. I usually get off at two. He said that I was to be at the beach in South Shore Park by one-thirty that afternoon. He said if I didn't show I would be in big trouble with Tony. He told me that I was to find Danny and buy some drugs. I didn't have any idea what it was about until I got to the beach."

"When Brooks first came to you at the warehouse, what was his mood?"

"He was excited, almost - - ah - - panicky. I'd never seen him like that before. He was always so cool and in control."

"What happened then?"

"I went to the beach and saw Danny like I was told. I met with him and bought some drugs. He told me that I was to go walking along the beach."

"Who told you?"

"Danny Minger."

"Did he say who told him to tell you that?"

"No, and I didn't ask. I did what I was told."

"Did you see anything strange on the beach that day?"

"I walked along the beach like I was told. A little while after I passed a vending cart, I saw the body at the edge of the water. I thought about running, but when I looked around and saw Lieutenant Brooks standing next to his car watching me, I sort of knew that I was supposed to find the girl."

"I can figure out what happened from there. What I want to know is who killed Robin Flower?"

"I don't know. I swear, I don't know," he said pleading that I would believe him.

I leaned back in the chair and looked at Ehman. I wasn't sure if I should believe him or not. Yet on the other hand, I was afraid that if I took him into protective custody he would end up like Danny. There had to be a better place, some place other than the jail to hide him.

"Do you have somewhere that you can hide, somewhere where Brooks or the Angelinis can't find you for a few days?"

"I have an aunt that lives out in Fox Point. I guess I could go there."

"Okay. I want you to go there and stay out of sight. Don't go outside, don't make any phone calls, don't let anyone know that your there. I'll get in touch with you later. Don't tell anyone where you're going, not even your mother. You're life depends on it. You understand me?"

"Yes, sir," he replied.

After I got the phone number and address of his aunt, I left him to explain things to his mother. I was hoping that I could keep him safe for at least a few days, hopefully until I could find out who I could trust and who I couldn't.

As I drove toward the Performing Arts Center to meet Monica for lunch, my mind was going at full speed in an effort to figure out how they got the body on the beach in broad daylight. Then I remembered that Jonathan had mentioned a vending cart. That was how it was done. It had to be.

At this point, I had a pretty good idea of who was involved and how the body had been dumped on the beach. The questions still to be answered were who killed her and why? I had my ideas, but it was another thing to prove it. It would take a lot more evidence than I had to get Captain Sinclair to question Brooks. I began to think that the most important question that I had to answer was who could I trust?

CHAPTER THIRTEEN

I drove to the Performing Arts Center and stopped out in front. I didn't see Monica anywhere around. A quick glance at my watch told me that I had arrived a few minutes early. Since I was stopped in a no parking zone, I drove down the block to a parking space and walked back to the front of the building where I leaned against one of the pillars to wait for her.

Time seemed to go by slowly as I watched the traffic and the people go by. Across the street there was an old lady pushing a shopping cart that must have had all her worldly possessions in it. I soon became fascinated with her and what she was doing.

By the time I checked my watch again, it was well past the time that Monica was to meet me. I looked around, but didn't see her. I was beginning to worry. I couldn't decide if I should simply continue to wait or if I should go inside and see if she was still there.

I was about to go inside to look for her when she came out the door. She had a big grin on her face as she sort of skipped down the steps toward me.

"You're late."

"I'm sorry, but I got us the greatest tickets to a play," she said as she waved them in front of me.

"What's the play?"

"Phantom of the Opera."

"Great. I've been wanting to see that."

"I'm glad. Where are we going to eat? I'm starving."

"Right over there," I said as I pointed to a café on the corner. "Great food."

Monica smiled as I took her by the arm and we walked to the corner. After crossing the street, we entered the little corner café. The smell of fresh baked bread mixed with the aroma of slow cooked barbecued roast filled the air.

The place was packed with the usual lunch crowd. It took a few minutes before we found a place to sit. I held the chair for Monica, then sat down across the little round table from her.

"Kind of a noisy place," she commented as she looked around the room.

"Yeah, but the food is out of this world."

"What would you recommend?"

"If you're really hungry, you might like their noon special, a barbecued beef sandwich," I suggested.

"Is that what you're going to have?"

"Yes, and a cup of coffee."

"Sounds good to me."

When the waitress came to the table, we gave her our order. While we waited, we talked about the play we were planning on seeing in a couple of days. Unfortunately, we were interrupted.

"Excuse me, but I would like to have a word with you."

I couldn't help but recognize that voice. Reluctantly, I turned and looked up to find Lieutenant Brooks standing beside the table.

"What do you want?" I asked bluntly.

Right now, he was the last person that I wanted to talk to, and from the look on Monica's face, she was not interested in talking to him, either.

"May I sit down?"

"No, I don't think so," I said flatly.

"I'm sure the lady won't mind," he said as he pulled out a chair.

"Oh, but you are mistaken. The lady does mind," Monica stated. "I mind very much."

Her reply set him back. He was not sure how to take such a straightforward rejection. I could not remember ever seeing Lieutenant Brooks so completely caught off guard.

"If you have something important to say to me, say it, then leave us alone," I said looking him in the eyes. "Otherwise, get lost."

Lieutenant Brooks looked at me as if he had forgotten what he was there for, but quickly recovered.

"Mr. Angelini would like to see you this afternoon at his warehouse on South Water Street."

"I saw Frank yesterday. If he wants to talk to me, he can call me at the office."

"Not Frank, Tony. And you'd better be there."

"Well, you've finally crawled out from under your rock into the daylight. I knew that you've been working for Angelini all the time. I just didn't have the right one. I must admit that it surprises me that you're so open about it."

"Listen you, if this wasn't a public place, I'd - - ."

"You'd what, Brooks? You're a dirty cop, and it won't be long before everyone will know it."

"You'll never be able to prove it," he said with a hard, cold stare. "You just be at the warehouse at two."

I watched Brooks as he turned and stormed out of the restaurant. I had to wonder what it was that had gotten him in so deep with the likes of Tony Angelini that he would sacrifice not only his career as a cop, but his honor and respect as well. The thought that he had sold his soul to the devil for a few pittances came to mind.

"Did you see the way he looked at you when you said he was a dirty cop? I think he wanted to kill you right here," Monica said, the tone of her voice showing how much the brief conversation with Brooks had upset her.

Monica may very well have been right, but I couldn't worry about that right now. What did Tony Angelini want to see me about? All I could think of was that he knew I had Ehman hidden away somewhere, and he was afraid of what

Ehman might say. He may have gotten to Danny Minger, but he was not going to get to Ehman, not if I could help it.

The thought crossed my mind that Lieutenant Brooks had more to fear by Ehman talking than Tony. Then the thought came to me. If it wasn't the police that Tony was afraid of, it had to be his father. Frank's form of justice for someone who disobeyed his rules was not only swifter, but it was much harsher than anything dished out by our legal system. Frank would not tolerate anyone going against him, not even his own son.

"I think Tony is afraid of his father," I said as I looked across the table at Monica. "I think Tony is afraid that his father would kill him if he ever finds out that his only son is addicted to drugs."

"You think that's why Tony wants to see you?"

"No. I think he wants to try to buy me off like he has Brooks and Wray."

"I don't think you should go to that warehouse," Monica said as she looked across the table at me.

The deep cobalt blue of her eyes did little to hide the concern she felt for my safety. She seemed to know that I would go to the warehouse no matter what she thought. She knew that I would meet with Tony Angelini, and that I would not give in to Tony's demands to forget about the investigation of the death of Robin Flower.

Nothing more was said for several minutes. I didn't have to be a mind reader to know that Monica was busy with thoughts of her own.

"Nick," she said softly. "I don't want you to go to that warehouse alone. If you must go, get some backup."

"If I take backup along, there will not be a meeting. I have to know what's on Tony's mind."

"It's not safe," she blurted out, then looked around the room as she realized that everyone close by could hear her.

"I have to go."

"Please, Nick," she pleaded softly.

"I have to go. I'll take you back to the apartment. You wait there. If I'm not back by, say, four, call Captain Sinclair and tell him everything," I instructed her.

Just then our lunches came. We ate, but my appetite was not up to the meal in front of me. From the looks of the way Monica ate, she was not as hungry as when we had sat down.

When we had eaten as much as we wanted, I paid the check and we left. I drove Monica back to my apartment. After making sure that she was safe inside, I drove to the warehouse on South Water Street.

The warehouse was built so that one side was along the lakefront. It was a fairly long building. As I drove up to it, I noticed how quiet it seemed to be. There was no one around. No cars, no trucks, no dockworkers, no nothing. I figured that Tony Angelini must have driven his car inside the building. I wouldn't think that Brooks would want his police car seen around here, so it was probably parked inside, too.

As I slowly drove along the building, a rather large man stepped out of one of the doors, looked around, and then flagged me to a stop. I watched him carefully as he walked toward my car. I didn't know him, but it was clear that he was a bodyguard, probably one of Tony's.

"Park your car over there, then come with me," he said.

I parked the car, got out, and followed him to a door. He opened the door and held it for me. I hesitated to go in, but this was not the time to change my mind. I was on my own, and I had no backup. It wasn't the smartest thing for me to do, but I was sure that it was the only thing I could do if I was to find Robin's killer.

I no more then stepped inside when I was greeted by two big thugs. They quickly took my gun and frisked me to make sure that I didn't have any other weapons.

I looked around the warehouse. It was empty except for three cars. One was a big Lincoln Town Car, which I was sure belonged to Tony. One was the dark blue sedan that

Brook's had been driving. The other was a large dark colored sedan that was probably used by Tony's goons.

The big man who had held the door didn't say anything, he simply pointed toward a small office in the corner of the warehouse. I walked toward the office, a goon on each side of me. When we got to the office, one of them opened the door and I stepped inside.

"Welcome, Detective McCord," Tony said with a smile as the door closed behind me.

A quick glance around the room revealed the presence of three other people. There were two of Tony's goons and Lieutenant Brooks.

"What's on your mind, Tony?" I asked casually.

"You have something I want very badly. Actually, you have a couple of things I want."

"What could I have that you would want?"

"You have a broach that belongs to my family, and I want it back. I also believe you have a letter. I want both of them."

"Sorry, but the broach is evidence."

"It may be evidence, but you checked it out of the morgue," Brooks said.

"You see, I know you have it," Tony added, his voice still rather pleasant and confident.

"I'm sure you will get it back after the investigation of the death of Robin Flower is over."

"You don't seem to understand. The investigation is already over," Tony said.

"The fact that a broach was found on Robin doesn't mean anything. The most it will do is show that you knew her, but we already know that. What is it you really want?"

"What you say is true. What I really want is the letter you found in Robin's apartment," Tony said.

"And Ehman," Brooks quickly added.

I noticed that Tony glanced over at Brooks. He had a disgusted look on his face. He didn't look too happy with Brooks at that moment. I wasn't sure why.

"What letter?" I asked as I looked back at Tony.

"Don't waste my time acting stupid. Wray saw Jerry with the letter, but he couldn't find it when he searched Jerry's office. He's sure Jerry doesn't have the letter any more. And if Jerry doesn't have the letter, then you must have it," Tony said.

I noticed that Tony was beginning to show signs of losing his patience. His voice was getting sharper, and there were little veins standing out on his neck.

"Just for the sake of argument, let's say that I have the letter. Why is it so important to you?"

"I didn't kill Robin. But if the contents of that letter gets to my father, well, you know him."

"We know you have the letter and we want it," Brooks demanded.

I glanced over at Brooks. He seemed more impatient to get a hold of the letter than Tony. I wondered why that was. What does he know, or thinks he knows about the letter. I couldn't remember anything in the letter that concerned anyone other than Tony. If I didn't know him any better, I would have thought there was something incriminating to Brooks in it.

"I didn't kill Robin," Tony insisted.

"You already said that," I replied. "Why should I believe you?"

"I cared for Robin," Tony said sharply.

"I believe you did, but something went very wrong. Am I right? Let me tell you what I think.

"I think Robin loved you very much, but you wouldn't give up the drugs. She told you that she would not marry you as long as you continued to use drugs. She probably told you that if you didn't stop using drugs, she would tell your father."

"Are you going to give me that letter?" Brooks demanded growing very impatient with me.

"No," I replied flatly.

"Well, I can see that it will be impossible to reason with you. I wonder how unreasonable you'll be when I have one of Tony's men pay a visit to that nice looking woman in your apartment," Brooks said with a nasty grin.

"You son of a b......."

I never got the chance to finish. I was instantly grabbed by two of Tony's gorillas. They shoved their guns into my ribs so hard that it doubled me over.

"Well, we're pretty tough," Brooks said with a stupid grin on his face.

"You harm one hair on her head and I will hunt you down. There won't be a sewer anywhere that you can crawl into and hide that I won't find you."

"I can see that this is getting us nowhere," Tony said in disgust.

"You want us to make fish bait out of him, boss," one of Tony's gorillas asked.

"Might as well. We're not going to get anywhere with him."

"Wait," Brooks shouted.

"What for?" Tony asked angrily.

"We still need him to tell us were he is hiding Ehman. We have to shut up Ehman," Brooks insisted.

"Ehman's your problem. You're a cop. You should be able to find him and take care of him," Tony said then turned to his goons.

"Get rid of him," Tony said to one of his goons as he stood up behind the desk.

"Damn it, Tony, think. He may have come down here alone, but I'll bet he told someone where he was going and who he was going to meet."

"You can bet on that," I said.

"If we kill him here, we'll have every cop in town all over this place. Your dad won't be very happy about that," Brooks added.

"Who would he have told?" Tony asked.

"The girl for one," Brooks answered as he looked at me.

I could tell he was thinking, wondering if I might have told anyone else. He knew that I had had time to tell someone else. He also knew that I had a lot of friends on the force, including Captain Sinclair, friends that would not interfere unless I disappeared.

"You're right, of course. We can't just kill a cop without causing a big mess, but we can't let him go, either," Tony said as he relented.

Tony's voice showed the panic that was starting to build inside him. He was beginning to understand the position that he had put himself in, and that there was little he could do to change it, now.

Tony began pacing back and forth behind the desk. I wondered what was going on in his head. He knew that it was not wise to kill me, but I was sure that he thought I knew too much for him to simply let me go.

Just then, another one of Tony's enforcers came in. Tony stopped pacing and looked at him.

"We got Charley, boss," the goon said.

Suddenly, Tony's face lit up. The look on his face told me that he had come up with an idea. He turned and looked at me.

"We're not going to kill you, but by this time tomorrow you won't be a cop. You won't be anything," Tony said with a sadistic grin.

"What do you have in mind?" Brooks asked.

"Bring Mitken in here," Tony ordered.

Two of Tony's goons dragged Charley into the room and dropped him in a chair. Charley had his hands tied behind his back. He turned pale when he saw me standing there.

"Honest, Tony, I never said a word to him. I wouldn't have talked," he pleaded.

"I know," Tony said calmly.

"Untie him," Tony said to one of his goons.

Charley was untied, but he remained seated in the chair. I had a bad feeling about this. Something was going to happen and I was the one who would come out on the short end of the stick.

"Give Brooks McCord's gun," Tony said.

Brooks looked a little surprised and confused, but didn't hesitate to take my gun from one of Tony's goons.

"Brooks, shoot Charley in the back of the head," Tony ordered.

"No, please, Mr. Angelini. I won't talk, honest," he begged as tears started to run down his face.

"I know you won't," Tony said, and then nodded toward Brooks.

Brooks moved up behind Charley while two of Tony's goons held him. Charley pleaded for his life as Brooks put my gun to the back of Charley's head. Brooks looked over at Tony. When Tony nodded, he pulled the trigger.

Suddenly, I felt a sharp pain at the back of my head. There were bright lights flashing in my eyes for just a split second, and then everything went black.

CHAPTER FOURTEEN

I thought I felt myself move, but I wasn't sure. Everything was a sort of a blur. My whole body seemed to ache, and the back of my head hurt something fierce. I felt as if I had been run over by a Mack truck. As the fog in my brain slowly started to clear, I realized I was lying on a cold concrete floor. I could not remember where I was or how I got there.

As I started to get up, what had happened began to creep back into my consciousness. I began to remember things, but only bits and pieces at first. I found I was able to stand up, but not without some difficulty. As I got to my feet, I sort of stumbled toward the desk and leaned on it for support.

I reached back and touched the tender knot on the back of my head. Pain shot through my head causing me to cringe. Once the pain subsided a little, I looked around the room. I stopped suddenly when I saw the body of Charley Mitken lying on the floor in a pool of blood. At the sight of him, I remembered what had taken place here, and how he was killed just before everything went blank.

It was when I heard the sounds of a siren in the background that it became very clear to me what was happening. Even with my brain clouded by the pain in the back of my head, I was able to understand that I had been set up to take the blame for the murder of Charley Mitken. It was then that I realized I was holding my gun in my hand.

"Drop the gun," a rather stern voice demanded.

I slowly turned and saw two uniformed officers standing in the door of the office with their guns pointed at me.

"I'm Detective Nick McCord," I said as I laid my gun on the desk and raised my hands.

The two officers entered the room, but didn't take their guns off me.

"My ID's in my inside coat pocket."

One of the officers carefully reached inside my coat and took out my ID while his partner kept a close eye on me. He looked at it, then at me.

"Sorry, sir. Can't be too careful."

"Yeah, I understand."

The other officer knelt down beside Charley. After checking to see if he was still alive, he turned and looked up at me. "This one's dead. Shot in the back of the head at close range."

The puzzled look on the officer's face as he looked at me gave me a hint of what he was thinking, and of what was to come. I thought about explaining what happened to him, but I realized what I had to say didn't sound very believable to me, why would it sound any better to him?

"You need to get hold of Captain Sinclair, that's Captain Joe Sinclair of the Park District, and the shooting team," I told the officers. "And don't touch anything."

I sat down in one of the chairs to wait, and to think about what had happened here. Brooks had shot Charley without so much as batting an eyelid. Although I knew that Brooks was a dirty cop, I never expected him to be a cold-blooded killer.

I couldn't worry about Brooks now. I had a more pressing problem at the moment. How was I going to explain this to Captain Sinclair, and how was I going to prove that I didn't shoot Charley? I just hoped that my head would clear enough so that I could make some sense of this to the captain.

It wasn't long before Captain Sinclair arrived, just minutes before the shooting team. Sinclair looked around the room, then at the body lying on the floor.

"What the hell have you gotten yourself into this time?" he asked as he walked across the room toward me.

"A real mess, Captain."

"I guess. Who shot Mitken?"

"Can we talk in private, Captain? After I tell you what happened, you can decide what to do next," I said.

"Sure," he replied, but he looked a little puzzled by my request and seemed a little reluctant to accommodate me.

Captain Sinclair followed me out of the office and into the warehouse. We walked over to a quiet corner and I leaned against the wall.

"Charley was shot with my gun, only I didn't pull the trigger. Lieutenant Brooks pulled the trigger," I said as I watched Captain Sinclair for his reaction.

"What?" he asked as he looked at me as if he didn't believe me. "I think you better explain this one in detail."

"Gladly."

I explained to Captain Sinclair how I happened to be in the warehouse in the first place, and what happened after I got there. I told him every little detail that I could remember right down to the cars parked inside the building, who was in the room, and what was said.

"Damn, Nick, you picked a fine time to go off by yourself. I'll get the shooting team to go over this place with a fine toothcomb. We'll look for tire tracks in the dirt on the floor, fingerprints, and anything else we can turn.

"I want you to go get your head looked at. When you get done, I want to see you in my office. I'll need your statement on everything you can remember as soon as possible. By the way, don't say a word about this to anyone, understand?"

"Yes, sir," I replied.

I walked out of the warehouse and over to my car. After getting in, I sat there thinking about what could happen to me if I couldn't prove my story to Captain Sinclair. Other than the fact that I could go to jail for killing Mitken, I knew that I would be suspended until a full investigation was completed. That would mean I would be taken off the Flower case. It suddenly all began to sink in. That was what Lieutenant Brooks and Tony Angelini wanted all along. That, and to get me out of the way.

I glanced at my watch. It reminded me that I needed to get back to my apartment. Monica would be worried, and I didn't want her finding out what had happened from anyone else.

I drove directly to my apartment. I spent the time driving home thinking about how I was going to explain all this to Monica. As I walked up the stairs, my head was throbbing. I slipped my key into the lock, unlocked the door and went in.

"Is that you, Nick?" Monica called from the kitchen.

"Yes," I replied as she stepped out of the kitchen to greet me.

From the quick change in the expression on her face, she must have realized that something was very wrong.

"Are you all right?" she asked as she hurried across the living room toward me.

"No. I took a nasty hit on the head. Would you mind getting me some aspirin?" I asked as I sank down on the sofa.

Monica went right to the bathroom and returned with the aspirin and a glass of water. After I took the aspirin, she sat down beside me. She didn't say anything. She just sat there looking at me. I could see the worried look on her face and knew that she wanted me to tell her what had happened.

I smiled in an effort to reassure her that everything was all right, then tipped my head back and closed my eyes. She sat quietly beside me as I waited for my headache to subside a little. Relaxing seemed to help some.

When I opened my eyes again, she was still sitting there. The worried look on her face told me that I needed to talk to her. I needed to explain what was going on.

"I'm in deep trouble, honey."

"What happened?"

I reached out and pulled her closer to me. As she curled up against me, I explained in detail what had happened at the warehouse. She continued to listen and didn't say anything as I rattled on about what could happen to me, but I could feel the tension in her body. It was obvious that it was upsetting to her.

"What happens now?" she asked calmly, although I knew she was anything but calm.

"I'll go down to the precinct and give my statement as to what happened and who was involved. Then, Captain Sinclair will suspend me and turn my case over to someone else. I will be sent home until an investigation is completed, during which time Internal Affairs will investigate my conduct."

"What will happen to you?"

"I think it's a little premature to start worrying about that. I have to get down to the precinct and give my statement while it's still fresh in my mind. After that, we'll have a quiet dinner and spend some time to ourselves," I said with a smile.

I was hoping that she wouldn't worry about what might happen. After all, I was worried enough for both of us.

As I got up, she stood up and put her arms around my neck. I wrapped my arms around her and looked down into her beautiful blue eyes, then leaned down and kissed her.

It felt so good to be in her arms and have her body pressed against me. The last thing I wanted to do was to leave her, but I had no choice.

"I've got to go," I said as I let go of her.

"I know," she sighed softly.

"I'll be back in a couple of hours, I hope."

"I'll be waiting," she said as I turned and started out the door.

As I got into my car, I noticed a dark blue sedan parked down the street. I wondered if it was the one with the missing hubcap. I also wondered if it would follow me or if whoever was in it was more interested in watching my apartment.

As I pulled out of the lot onto the street, the car pulled away from the curb. I made a turn at the end of the next block to see if it was following me. As it followed me around the corner, I noticed it was not the one with the missing hubcap.

I kept an eye on it as I led it away from my apartment. It followed me until I was within a few blocks of the police building, then turned off. I had to wonder if I was being tailed at the request of Captain Sinclair. I didn't think he would order a tail on me yet, but I could understand why he would under the circumstances.

Once I arrived at the police building, I went directly to Captain Sinclair's office to make my statement. He was sitting at his desk. There was another officer with him. I immediately recognized the officer as Sergeant Mike Morris from Internal Affairs. I knew what was to happen next. I knocked on the captain's door.

"Come in, Nick."

I opened the door and walked in.

"I believe you know Sergeant Morris with Internal Affairs," Sinclair said.

"Yes. Good to see you, Mike."

"I'm sorry our meeting has to be under such circumstance."

"Me, too."

"Well, gentleman, shall we get started," Captain Sinclair interrupted, then reached over and turned on a small tape recorder.

I looked at Captain Sinclair. Even though I knew it was routine in cases like this, I still found it rather disturbing.

"First of all, Nick, I have to ask you if you want an attorney present?" Mike asked.

"Am I under arrest?" I asked with surprise.

"No, but what you say here can be used against you in a court of law if charges are filed against you," Mike reminded me.

"I know my rights and I'll be telling you the truth. I don't need an attorney to do that," I said with a little more anger in my voice than I had intended.

"Okay, then," Mike said. "If you change your mind at anytime, we will stop until you can get an attorney. We will be recording your statement. After it is typed up, you will have a chance to read it before you sign it. Is that understood?"

"Yes," I replied.

"Good. I would like you to start by explaining how you happened to be in that warehouse in the first place. Then, I want you to tell us what happened, in the order it happened, to the best of your ability."

I noticed that Mike had become very professional, but that was his job. His job was to get to the truth.

I began by telling them about Brooks coming to me at the café to tell me that Tony Angelini insisted on seeing me at the warehouse.

"Do you have a witness to your meeting with Lieutenant Brooks in the café?" Mike asked.

"It wasn't a meeting. I was not there to see Brooks. Brooks came up to me while I was having lunch. And, yes, I have a witness."

"Who?" Mike asked.

I glanced over at Captain Sinclair. He knew that I was at the café with Monica, but didn't say anything.

"I'll tell you that if I think it's necessary. Would you like me to go on?" I asked sharply.

"Yes," Mike replied.

I continued by taking it step by step. I told them everything that was done and everything that was said right up until Captain Sinclair arrived on the scene.

"You're trying to tell us that Lieutenant Brooks shot Charley Mitken in the back of the head with your gun right in front of you?" Mike asked, the expression on his face indicating that he found it hard to believe what I had told him.

"That's what I said, and that's what I meant," I replied, making every effort to keep my voice as calm as I could.

"He shot him right in front of you?"

"Yes."

I was getting the impression that they were a long way from believing me. As I thought about it, I would have had a hard time believing me, too. Assassinating someone is bad enough, but doing it in front of witnesses is not a wise move on anyone's part. I knew Brooks was not a stupid man. Greedy, maybe, but not stupid.

"All I can say is Lieutenant Brooks shot Charley Mitken in the back of the head with my gun while I watched. There wasn't a damn thing I could do about it. I had a couple of Tony's goons with guns on me. I think I had enough to worry about at that moment without worrying about Lieutenant Brooks."

Mike continued to ask the same questions over and over. It was routine, but I was getting a bit tired of it. Each time he asked a question, he got the same answer. I was getting a little irritated with the questions being repeated again and again when I had been telling them the truth from the beginning. It certainly didn't help any that my head was throbbing and I was tired. It also didn't help any that my whole career was on the line and it wasn't looking very good for me. I knew that all the evidence would be pointing right at me. It was my gun that did the killing. I was the only one, other than Charley, in the building when the police arrived.

They were sure that they had caught me with the "smoking gun", so to speak, in my hand.

"You said that Lieutenant Brooks wants you off the Robin Flower case so the case will be turned over to him, is that correct?"

"That's what I said. How many times do I have to say things before you start understanding what I'm telling you?"

I took a deep breath and looked over at Captain Sinclair. I wanted to tell him to make Mike back off, but I knew Mike was only doing his job. I would have done the same thing if I had been in his shoes.

"Look, Mike. I know what you're trying to do. I want the same thing you want, the truth. Well, you're getting the truth from me. What you'll get when you question Brooks, God only knows."

"You're making one hell of an accusation against a cop with an outstanding record. What kind of proof do you have?" Mike asked.

"I don't have any, - - yet," I admitted.

"Then how the hell are we supposed to believe you," Captain Sinclair said with a tone of frustration.

"I guess I wouldn't believe me, either," I said feeling frustrated.

"Why do you think Brooks wants you off the Flower case?" Mike asked again.

"I'm not really sure. At first, I thought it was because the case was too close to the Angelini family, but now I'm not so sure. Now, I think that he wants control of the case so he can control what information gets out to the public."

"You mean so he can leak out information?" Mike asked.

"Not so much so he can leak out information, but more so he can hide information. Specifically, a letter written by Robin Flower to Frank Angelini."

"What's in the letter?" Captain Sinclair asked.

"I'd rather not say at this time. It may be my only ace in the deck."

"Nick, I'm not going to be able to help you if you don't confide in me," Captain Sinclair said.

"Captain, I know you're trying to help me. I need some time to put together my thoughts on what I really have and what I can prove. Right now, my head is splitting so bad that I can hardly think."

"Okay," Captain Sinclair conceded.

"But - - ," Mike said as he started to object, but was quickly cut off by Captain Sinclair.

"We've got his statement. That will be all for now. I'll set up another chance for you to question Nick when he's feeling better," Captain Sinclair said to Mike.

Mike knew that it was over for him. It would do him no good to press the issue with Captain Sinclair. He was out ranked and he knew when he was being dismissed.

"I'll need to talk to you again," Mike said.

"Sure," I replied. "Maybe, I'll feel better tomorrow."

Mike nodded, then left Sinclair's office with a disgusted look on his face. I was almost sure that he had planned to drill me for hours. At least until he was totally convinced that I was either telling him the truth, or he was convinced that he couldn't get me to change my story.

I knew it wasn't over between the Captain and me, either. He had his duty, too.

"You know I have to suspend you and take your gun and shield. I don't like doing this, but its regulations."

"I know," I replied as I handed him my gun and badge.

"You are on suspension with pay until this investigation is over. Go home and get some rest. By the way, stay out of trouble for once."

"Yes, sir."

"And Nick, don't be hard to get in touch with. If we can't get in touch with you, it won't look good."

I nodded that I understood, then left his office. I went to my desk and picked up the note pad that I had been using to make notes on my suspects. It would provide a quick reference to what I had found out about each of them.

After getting in my car, I noticed the dark blue sedan with the missing hubcap was parked in the spaces reserved for police cars. I was about to start my car when I noticed Bob Wray come out of the building with an official looking envelope in his hand. He walked up to the car and unlocked the door. As he opened the door, he looked around as if to see if anyone was watching him. He got in the car and drove out of the garage.

From his actions, I got the feeling that he was sneaking out with something that he wasn't supposed to be taking out of the station. I decided to start my car and follow him out onto the street.

Wray only drove about four blocks before he pulled over and parked at the curb. He got out of his car and walked across the street to a small café. I wondered if he was just going to get something to eat or if he was meeting someone there. I noticed that he took the envelope with him. I decided that it might be advantageous to find out what he was doing.

I parked my car, then walked across the street. I snuck up to the window of the café and looked inside. I couldn't see who was in the booth, but I watched Wray as he stood next to the table. I saw a man's hand reach out. Wray handed the man the large yellow envelope. They talked for a minute or so, then Wray turned to leave. I ducked around the corner and waited until Wray got back in his car and left.

I waited for a couple of minutes in the hope that the other man would come out and I would get a chance to see who he was, but no one left. I decided to go into the café and find out who the man was that Wray had given the envelope to. I walked back to the front of the café and went inside. I looked over at the booth where the man had been, but it was empty. I took a quick look around, but didn't see anyone I recognized. The man must have slipped out the back way, and that it would be too late for me to see who it was.

As I walked back to my car, I wondered who it was that had been in the café. Was it Lieutenant Brooks? Possibly, Tony Angelini? Maybe someone else?

I quickly decided that it was not going to do me any good to stand around there guessing. I got back in my car and drove to my apartment.

When I arrived at my apartment, Monica was waiting for me at the door. The look on her face told me that she had been worried. She took hold of my hand and walked with me to the sofa.

"You want to talk about it?" she asked softly as I sat down on the sofa.

She curled up beside me as I told her what happened in Captain Sinclair's office. I gave her some idea of what we could expect and explained the process used by Internal Affairs. It was nice to have someone to talk to and to share my feelings. She was very attentive.

I was hungry and had not had anything to eat since lunch. Monica had fixed dinner so we sat down to eat. We discussed what had happened in Captain Sinclair's office some more. After dinner, we cleaned up the kitchen together and continued to talk about what it meant for me to be suspended.

"What happens now that you are suspended?"

"Nothing. I don't have to get up and go to work. I don't have to do anything I don't want to do, at least until they decide they want to talk to me again. At this point, it's wait and see."

"What do we do now, I mean right now?" she asked.

"I'm pretty tired, it's been a long day. I would like to go to bed, if you don't mind."

"I don't mind, if you don't mind if I come to bed with you."

"I was hoping you would say that," I said as I stood up and reached out a hand for her.

It wasn't long before we were in bed. She curled up against me and rested her head on my shoulder. The feel of her warm body against me helped relax the tensions of the day and clear my mind. Just having her in my arms was enough to make me feel better. I soon found myself off in dreamland, getting the rest I needed. It was the kind of rest that would allow me to think more clearly, and to face the days ahead.

CHAPTER FIFTEEN

I woke to the sound of thunder crashing in the distance. I could hear the rain outside my window. It was still dark outside and I wasn't sure if it was because of the dark gray morning, or if it was still too early for the sun to be up. I didn't want to disturb Monica in order to see my clock, so I lay quietly. Monica was curled up against my back. The feel of her warm body against me made me want to stay right there all day. I closed my eyes in the hope of returning to sleep.

My mind soon filled with thoughts of yesterday, so many thoughts that I found sleep impossible. This was the first time that my integrity as a police office had come into question by anyone, and it bothered me. It was just soaking in as to what that really meant to me.

I had leveled some pretty strong charges against a fellow police officer who just happened to have an impeccable service record. It was something that I didn't take lightly. Even though I had seen him commit the crime I had accused him of, now I was going to have to prove it. If I could prove it, I would be able to save my own skin, to say nothing of saving my career.

I was convinced that my only hope lay in Jonathan Ehman. He would be the one person who could help me prove that Lieutenant Brooks was a dirty cop. He also might be able to indicate that he was involved in the death of Robin Flower. It was time that I had a serious talk with Jonathan. It was time to force him to tell me everything he knew about Lieutenant Brooks and Tony Angelini.

Then, there was Bob Wray. I was also convinced that he was Lieutenant Brooks's eyes and ears. His snitch, in other words. Wray had been driving the car with the missing hubcap most of the time, if not all the time. He had been the one following me around, leaking information from the lab and keeping tabs on all of the evidence in the Flower murder case. He was passing what he learned on to Lieutenant Brooks, I was sure of it.

I had to wonder if Wray was the one who killed Danny. If he had killed him, how did he get it done? How was he able to get the right hot dogs to Danny? The most logical answer was that he had help from someone in the jail kitchen, but who? Some of the workers in the jail kitchen were prisoners. That could explain how he knew which hot dogs to inject with the anesthetic.

The feel of a soft warm hand that slid around from my side to my chest pleasantly interrupted my thoughts. The light kiss on the back of my neck along with her warm breath on my ear quickly turned my attention to the body curled up against my back.

"What are we going to do today? We have the whole day all to ourselves," she whispered in my ear.

"Not quite. I have to find out who killed Robin Flower."

"You've been suspended. Let someone else find out who killed her," Monica said softly.

"Honey, if I can find out who killed Robin, I might be able to prove that Lieutenant Brooks shot Charley. I'm sure that it's all connected somehow. It has to be."

I knew that if it wasn't connected, then it would be the end for me. That could very well mean that I could go to jail for a very long time.

"Okay, where do we start?" she asked after she took a moment to think about what I said.

It was clear to me that Monica was not going to let me go anywhere alone. I guess I really couldn't blame her. After all, the last time I went somewhere alone I ended up under suspicion of murder and the prime, if not the only, suspect.

"We start with breakfast," I said. "Then we're going to Fox Point to see Jonathan Ehman. I think he knows more than he's telling me."

"Where's Fox Point?"

"It's up north along the shore."

Monica scooted over as I rolled onto my back. She rolled up over me, stretching her naked body over me and we kissed. Her warm firm breasts pressed against my chest. She rose up on her elbows and looked down at me. A soft smile came over her face.

"Nick," she whispered softly. "No matter what happens, I want you to know that I love you. And I know you didn't kill Charley."

"I love you, too. You have no idea how important it is to me that you know I didn't kill him and that you believe in me," I said and then pulled her back over me for another kiss.

After a few more kisses and a little touching of each other, we managed to get out of bed and get dressed. By the time we had had breakfast, it was getting a little lighter outside. I could still hear the rain against the windows and the occasional rumble of thunder off in the distance.

We left my apartment and went to the garage for the car. As I backed out of the garage, I glanced in the rearview mirror. I noticed a plain looking sedan parked across the street. I didn't see anyone in the car and began to think that I might be getting a little paranoid. Paranoid or not, I was not about to be followed. The last thing I wanted to do was lead the police, or anyone else for that matter, to the one person who might be able to help me.

I drove out onto the street, then made a quick turn at the next corner, then another quick turn into an alley and stopped. It was less then a minute before the sedan I'd seen parked across the street turned into the alley and stopped only twenty or so feet from me. Behind the wheel was a rather embarrassed police officer. From the look on his face, he knew that he had been caught tailing me.

I opened the door and stepped out of the car. As I walked back toward the police car, I recognized the driver. He rolled down the window and waited for me to come to him.

"I'm sorry, Nick. I have my orders," he said apologetically.

"I'm sorry, too, Martin. I was hoping that it wasn't going to come to this."

"We've known each other since the police academy and we've been good friends for years. I don't like this any more than you do."

"I need you to do me a favor."

"Come on, Nick. Don't ask me not to follow you. You know I can't do that."

"I'm not going to ask you not to follow me. I'm asking you to follow me onto Interstate 94. After you've followed us for a while, call in and tell them that we left town. You could suggest that I must be taking Miss Barnhart back to Madison."

"They won't buy that."

"Maybe, maybe not. All I really need is a little time."

Martin sat in the car and looked out the windshield. I was sure that he was thinking about what he should do. I was asking a lot of him.

"Okay, but you have to make it look like you're leaving town," he said as he looked at me.

"No problem, follow me down interstate 94 to the city limits, then turn off and call in."

Martin nodded that he understood. I didn't say any more. I turned around and walked back to my car. I got in and started to drive toward Interstate 94 with Martin only a short distance behind me.

Monica didn't say a word, she watched Martin in the outside rearview mirror. Every once in a while she would glance over at me. I think she wanted to ask me what was going on, but didn't. I felt she should know what I was doing.

"We're going out of town toward Madison. Martin will turn off after we leave the city limits. Then we'll swing around and work our way to Fox Point."

"Why are we going to all that trouble? Why doesn't he just say he lost us and return to the police station?"

"Because I don't want him to get into trouble. Martin is too good a cop. This way when he reports that we left town, he won't be lying and he'll stay out of trouble. Another thing is he may very well be followed, too. I'm sure that whoever put him on my tail knows that we have been friends for a long time."

We cruised down the Interstate keeping Martin in sight behind us. Shortly after we left the city limits, Martin turned off the Interstate. We got off at the next exit and began working our way north and east, to make sure that we didn't have someone else tailing us.

Once we got to Fox Point, it took us only a few minutes to find the street that Ehman's aunt lived on. I remembered the last time I tried to talk to Ehman and the chase that followed. I had no desire to chase him again.

"When we get to the house, I want you to go to the front door and ask for Ehman. I'll go to the back of the house, just in case he tries to run again," I said as I pulled up in front of the driveway to block it off.

As soon as I stopped the car, I got out and started up the driveway to the back of the house while Monica went to the front door. Just as I stepped around the back of the house, I heard Monica knock on the door. I heard someone answer the door, but I could not hear what was being said. Suddenly the back door flew open and Jonathan came running out.

"Stop right there," I yelled. "I'm not going to chase you this time."

Jonathan stopped, looked back at me and saw me leaning against the house. From the look on his face, he was trying to decide if he should run or give it up.

"You run and I'll shoot your legs out from under you," I said as I slid my hand under my coat.

He looked at me, then at my coat. I could tell he was trying to decide if I meant what I said or if I was bluffing.

"Go ahead, try me," I dared him.

Jonathan's shoulders sagged as he let out a long sigh and began walking toward me.

"Good decision. Now, we need to talk."

I followed Jonathan back into the house. We went into the kitchen and were soon joined by Monica and his aunt. Monica sat down next to me and across the table from Jonathan's aunt.

"I'm Betty Ehman, Jonathan's aunt. I take it you're Detective McCord?"

"Yes. This is Monica Barnhart."

"I would like to be here while you question him, if you don't mind. We've talked quite a bit since he came to stay with me. Jonathan would like to help you in anyway he can, sort of clean the slate, so to speak."

It was clear that Aunt Betty was not going to put up with her nephew lying to the police. She was insisting on him coming clean with everything. I really thought that she could see the good in him and wanted him to start down the right path, for a change.

"Thank you. Jonathan, I need to know all you can tell me about Lieutenant Brooks, Tony Angelini, and Bob Wray."

I noticed that the mention of Bob Wray caused Jonathan to flinch a little. I wondered what caused that, but I could wait to find out.

"Let's start with Lieutenant Brooks."

"I told you about Lieutenant Brooks."

"Yes, you did. But I think there's more. Brooks didn't enlist you just to buy drugs from Danny to give to Tony, did he?"

"No," he admitted softly. "Lieutenant Brooks had me watching everything that Mr. Angelini did. Mr. Angelini did all his business at the warehouse, and a lot of it at night. I was supposed to watch everyone who came to the warehouse, how long they stayed, what they did, and anything else I could find out, then report it to Lieutenant Brooks."

"I take it we're talking about Tony Angelini?"

"Yeah."

"Who came to see Angelini, say in the last few weeks?"

"Charley Mitken came one night, the night Robin Flower was killed. He and Tony had kind of a heated argument. I heard Tony tell Charley that he would have a visitor if he talked," Ehman said.

"Talked about what?"

"I don't know. I got the impression that Tony had Mitken do a job for him."

"What kind of job?"

"I think Tony was trying to put some pressure on a couple of drug dealers, but I'm not sure. It could have been something else."

"Was Danny one of them that Tony wanted to put pressure on?"

"I don't know, could be."

"If you want me to help you, you have to tell Mr. McCord everything," his aunt said.

Jonathon looked at his aunt, then looked at me. After taking a minute to think, he continued.

"Yeah. He had Danny pretty scared. I saw Danny at the park the day I found the body."

"Tell me what happened that day."

"I got a call from Lieutenant Brooks. He told me that I was to go to South Shore Park. I was to be there by one o'clock at the latest. I was to buy cocaine from Danny for Mr. Angelini. Danny was to tell me what to do then.

"Danny told me to hang around until a body showed up on the beach. As soon as I saw the body, I was to call the police. I figured that I would be able to disappear after I called the police, but Lieutenant Brooks kept me there until you arrived."

"Why?"

"I don't know."

I had to think about that for a moment. What possible reason could Brooks have for keeping Jonathan at the scene? It was possible that Jonathan didn't know why Brooks wanted him to hang around. If that was the case, then I would have to find that out from Brooks.

"Who else came to see Tony at the warehouse?"

"Joe Martonie came by a few days before Robin died. Tony had some ugly things to say to him."

"Like what?"

"Tony accused Joe of flirting with Robin when he wasn't looking, and trying to get Robin to have an affair with him. Joe liked Robin, and I think Robin liked Joe. But there was nothing between them."

"Did Robin ever spend any time alone with Joe?" Monica asked.

I knew what she was getting at. She was thinking that Robin was killed because of Tony's jealousy, and she might be right.

"I heard that there had been a party at Frank Angelini's house. Some time during the party, Robin and Joe went down by the pool. I heard Joe insist that all they did was sit and talk, but Tony came unglued and screamed that Joe was not to so much as look at Robin ever again if he valued his life.

"Tony was pretty jealous of anyone who talked to or even looked at Robin. I remember one time when Robin got really mad at Tony and accused him of smothering her, and not allowing her to have any friends."

"Did Travis Fox ever come to the warehouse?" I asked.

"Yeah, but it was a long time ago. Maybe a year ago or more."

"What happened?"

"I remember that Mr. Fox came in madder than hell. He told Tony that he was not going to work for him any more. I heard him say that if Tony ever tried to drag him into any of his dirty dealings again, he would tell Tony's father that he was using his own product. Mr. Fox said he was going straight, and he never wanted to see the likes of Tony, or his enforcers again."

I had to wonder if maybe Travis had done just what he said he was going to do. I hadn't seen so much as a parking ticket in his file for the past eighteen months or so.

"What's Travis doing, besides working in the jewelry store?"

"Nothing that I know of," Jonathan replied. "I haven't seen him since that night."

"What can you tell me about Bob Wray?"

Jonathan looked at his aunt as if he were hoping that she would not make him say anything about Wray to me.

"Tell him, Jonathan," his aunt insisted.

From the look on Jonathan's face, he didn't want to say anything about Wray. I got the idea that he was more afraid of Wray than of anyone else.

"What is it about Wray that has you so scared?" I asked.

Jonathan hesitated to answer.

"Tell him, Jonathan," his aunt insisted again.

"It's not so much what I've seen, but more of what I've heard."

"What have you heard?"

"I overheard Lieutenant Brooks tell Tony that Wray had taken care of one of Tony's loose ends, and that he did it with pleasure. The next day I heard that Danny died in jail while he was being held under protective custody. I can tell you that scared me. I knew that I would be next, if I talked to the police."

"That's why I sent you here. I needed to be sure you would be safe. I couldn't be sure of that if you were in jail. What can you tell me about Robin's death?"

"I don't know who killed her, if that's what you're asking."

I looked at him as I thought about what Jonathan had told me. Spending any more time questioning him now was not likely to add anything to what he had already said. If I thought of something else, I could call him later.

"Okay. That's all I have for now. This is my private number," I said as I gave him a card. "You call me if you think of anything, anything at all that will help me find Robin's killer."

"I heard on the news this morning that you were suspended pending an investigation of the shooting death of Charley Mitken in the warehouse. Is that true?"

"Yes, it is. But I didn't kill him."

"Do you know who did?"

"Yes, but I can't prove it, yet. When I do, I believe that I will also know who killed Robin Flower," I said.

"I want you to stay here with your aunt. Don't talk to anyone and don't go anywhere. I'll be in touch," I added.

Monica and I said goodbye to Jonathan and his aunt and walked out to the car. After we got in, Monica looked over at me.

"Do you think he's telling the truth?"

"I think so," I replied. "He's scared. He's trying to get out of all this with his skin still intact."

"Why didn't you tell him who killed Charley?"

"He's scared enough. If I tell him that Lieutenant Brooks killed him, he might not talk, or worse, he might try to run. If he tries to run, he's not likely to live very long. As long as no one knows where he is, he's safe. The minute someone sees him out in public, he's dead."

Monica said nothing more as I started the car and pulled away from the curb. We were both deep in thought as I headed back toward Milwaukee.

Jonathan had given me a little more to go on. I was now more convinced than ever that Wray had killed Danny, and now I had a good idea as to who gave the order. It was beginning to look more and more like Brooks and Wray did most of the dirty work for Tony Angelini.

I remembered what Frank Angelini had told me about turning over the person who killed Robin to him. I wondered what Frank would think if I told him that Robin's killer was his own son, or was it? What about Travis Fox? I still wasn't sure how he fit into this.

Monica suddenly interrupted my thoughts.

"Nick, I was thinking. If Tony killed Robin in a jealous rage, why was she shot in the back of the head?"

"I don't know," I replied as I continued to think about it.

There were still several loose ends floating around. As I went over all that had happened in the past couple of days, I remembered that Monica and I had not returned to Robin's apartment to check on the rest of the jewelry that had been stashed in the hidden drawer in the bottom of the jewelry chest.

Remembering the jewelry chest also reminded me of the reaction we got from Travis Fox when Monica showed him the pin with the small "C" on the crest. It made me wonder where he disappeared to that afternoon.

"I think we need to talk to Mr. Travis Fox again," I said almost as if I was thinking out loud.

"You think he's got something to do with all this?"

"I don't know for sure. But if he doesn't, he might know something that will help."

"Do you think he will talk to us?"

"I don't know, but it's worth a try. But first, we need to stop by my apartment and call Sam Kishler. He might have found out something about that pin. We also need to go to Robin's apartment and check on that hidden jewelry."

"I forgot about that," Monica said. "Nick, do you think it's safe to return to your apartment. The police are probably just waiting for you to return. They might have your phone bugged, too."

"You have a point there. Let's go to a motel. We can get a room and make our call from there."

"Since we need to stop at Robin's apartment, maybe the phone in her apartment is still hooked up and we could call Sam from there."

This was one smart lady I had gotten hooked up with. I turned the car off the Interstate and headed toward Robin's apartment in the Kilbourn District.

CHAPTER SIXTEEN

As we entered the Kilbourn District of the city, it occurred to me that Robin's apartment might still be under surveillance. It was important that I not be seen going in or out of her apartment. If I got caught working on the investigation of Robin's murder, I could be arrested and charged with breaking regulations. That would do little to help me clear myself of any wrongdoing. There would be little I could do for myself if I was sitting in jail.

I turned onto a street that ran parallel to the street Robin's apartment was on, but two blocks north. I pulled into the small parking lot of a local grocery store and parked toward the back, away from the street, to reduce the possibility that my car would be spotted.

"What are we doing here?" Monica asked.

"We're leaving the car here and walking to Robin's apartment," I replied.

"But it's raining," she reminded me.

"It's not raining very hard, just sprinkling a little. You can wait here if you want."

"No. I'm not letting you out of my sight. I'll come with you," she said as she got out of the car. "Do you think the police are still watching Robin's apartment?"

"I don't know, but I'm not taking any chances."

I took Monica's hand and started down the street. It was a little cooler than it had been the past few days. The fresh smell of a warm summer rain filled the air, and the cool droplets of water on my face felt good. Unfortunately, I could not enjoy it like I had so many times in the past. I had too much on my mind. In fact, my whole future was on my mind. However, it did help a little to have Monica's hand in mine.

As we approached the street where Robin's apartment was located, I hesitated. Monica looked at me. I'm sure she was wondering what was going on in my head.

"Wait here. I'm going to see if anyone is watching the place."

I let go of Monica's hand and walked along the tall hedge of lilac bushes. I kept an eye out for any cars that even remotely resembled a police car as I approached the end of the hedge, but I didn't see any.

When I got to the end of the hedge, I stepped up close to it. I slowly pushed a branch out of the way so I could see around the end of the hedge. There it was as I was sure it would be. At the other end of the block sat a dark colored sedan. I studied it for several minutes before I was able to detect movement inside the car. Someone was sitting in it. I was sure they were keeping the apartment building under surveillance to see who came and went.

Just as I was about to turn around to let Monica know what I had seen, another dark colored sedan came around the corner and stopped behind the first car. I continued to watch as the driver of the second car got out. He took a minute to look around. That's when I recognized him. It was Bob Wray.

He walked up to the first car and leaned down by the driver's window. They talked for a minute or so, but I was too far away to hear anything.

Within a few minutes, Wray stepped back away from the first car. It pulled away from the curb and came toward me. I quickly turned and motioned for Monica to duck behind the hedge as I ran toward her. I no more then got behind the hedge with her when the car went past the corner.

I was sure that we had not been seen, but it had been close. In my effort to keep from being seen, I had not had a chance to see who was in the car.

"Did you see who was in the car?"

"No," Monica replied.

We waited for several minutes, but the second car did not go by. I left Monica and carefully worked my way back to the end of the hedge. As I again peered around the hedge, I could see Wray sitting in his car. It looked like he might be settling in for a long wait, probably for me. I turned around and walked back to where Monica waited.

"Looks like Bob Wray is taking his turn at standing watch. We'll have to go in the back."

"Won't they be watching the back?"

"I doubt it. You have to have a pass key to get in from the back," I said with a grin as I held up the key that I had kept from my last visit to Robin's apartment.

"Sneaky," Monica said with a grin.

I took Monica's hand again as we started down the alley behind the apartments. We walked past the garages and followed a tree lined walk to the rear entrance. I slipped the key into the lock and opened the door. As I held the door for Monica, I looked around to see if anyone was nearby who could see us enter the building. I didn't see anyone.

I led Monica to the second floor and down the hall to Robin's apartment. The bright yellow police tape still sealed the door. After unlocking the door, I pushed it open and held the tape up for Monica. She ducked under it. I followed her into the apartment after a quick check to make sure that the hall was clear and that no one had seen us enter the apartment.

Monica went straight to the bedroom. I followed her. She opened the bottom of the freestanding jewelry chest. Her face lit up as she looked up at me and smiled.

"It's still here," she said softly.

"All of it?"

"Yes. I'm a little surprised that your lab people didn't find it."

"So am I."

"What do you want me to do?"

"Finish sketching what is there so we can identify it later, if we have to. I'll check to see if the phone still works."

Monica began sketching the remaining jewelry while I went into the living room. There was a phone in the bedroom, but I didn't want to disturb Monica.

I picked up the phone and discovered that it still had a dial tone. I called the number Monica had given me for the History Department of the University of Wisconsin. The phone rang a couple of times before it was answered.

"University of Wisconsin, History Department. How may I direct your call?" a pleasant female voice asked.

"I would like to speak to a Sam Kishler, please."

"Is he expecting your call?"

"No, well yes. I'm calling for Doctor Barnhart."

"Just one moment."

I waited for a minute, not sure if she was going to put me through to Doctor Kishler, or leave me on hold until I gave up.

"I'm sorry, Doctor Barnhart is not in."

"I know that, she is here with me. I want to talk to Doctor Kishler."

"Just a minute," she said, sounding just a little disgusted with me.

"This is Doctor Kishler."

"Doctor Kishler, I'm Nick McCord - - ."

"Oh, Monica's friend," he said with a hint of excitement in his voice.

"Yes. Did you get a chance to look at the pictures of the pin we sent you?"

"Yes. Yes, I did. It's a very interesting pin."

"Yes, it is. What can you tell me about it?"

"Well, it was made in Italy, probably around the eighteen forties to the eighteen sixties. The crest belongs to the Cermona family and dates back hundreds of years. I'm afraid that's about all I can tell you about it without actually seeing it. It is very rare and I suspect that it is rather valuable. It is probably one of the very few pieces of jewelry left in existence made by that particular craftsman."

"We have another piece of jewelry made by the same craftsman that belongs to a different family."

"Really? That's interesting."

"I want to thank you for your help. It was kind of you to take the time."

"I'm always willing to help the police and a friend of Monica's. Will you tell Monica that we miss her and hope she will return soon?"

"Sure will. Thanks again," I said, then hung up the phone.

I sat down on the arm of one of the large chairs. My thoughts returned to Travis Fox and his reaction to the pin. I wondered why Fox was so interested in that particular piece of jewelry? My first thought was that it was because of its value, but that didn't seem to be the answer. He had access to a lot of valuable jewelry, both old and new. There had to be more to it than its monetary value.

My thoughts were suddenly interrupted by the sound of someone at the door. It didn't sound like someone with a key. It was more like the sound of someone picking the lock.

I ran into the bedroom. Monica looked up at me with a surprised look on her face. I could see that she was about to say something, but stopped when I put my finger over my mouth.

She grasped the message quickly and closed the secret door to the jewelry chest and stood up. I motioned for her to duck into the closet while I ducked behind the door.

I heard the door open and someone come into the apartment. I tried to peek through the crack between the door and its frame, but all I could make out was a well-dressed man with the collar of his expensive raincoat turned up. My first thought was that it might be Lieutenant Brooks, but I quickly realized that it was not him. He wouldn't have had to pick the lock, he would have access to a key. After he looked around, he turned and started toward the bedroom. It was then that I saw who it was. It was Travis Fox.

I waited behind the door until he walked into the bedroom. He went directly to the jewelry chest. As he knelt down to open the secret drawer, I swung the bedroom door shut.

When he heard the door close, he turned and looked at me. He seemed very surprised to see me standing there watching him.

"Looking for something, Fox?" I asked.

"What are you doing here?"

"Looking for clues to Robin's death. Again, what are you doing here?"

He let out a long sigh and looked down at the floor. I wasn't sure what he was going to do, but I got the impression that he wasn't going to give me a hard time. He looked more like a man who had decided it was time to get whatever he knew off his chest and to come clean.

"You mind if I sit on the bed? I'm not carrying a gun," he said, his voice indicating a resignation.

"No, not at all. Let's relax while you explain why you're here."

Travis sat down on the edge of the bed with his hands on his knees. He looked down at the floor for a minute before looking up at me again. He let out a long sigh before speaking.

"I came to get some jewelry that I had loaned Robin, - - Miss Flower. The place has been crawling with cops, up until now. This was the first chance I've had to see if any of it was still here and hopefully get it back."

As Monica came out of the closet, Travis turned and watched her move across the room. She sat down on a chair next to the dresser while I leaned against the door.

"You're the woman who brought that old pin into the jewelry store," he said, obviously surprised to see her in Robin's apartment.

"Yes," Monica replied.

"Where did you get it?"

"We found it here in Robin's apartment," I replied. "What is the pin to you?"

He looked at me for a minute before responding.

"The pin belonged to my grandmother. I believe that it originally belonged to her mother. It has been in my family for many years. I would like to have it back."

"If it was so valuable to you, why did you give it to Robin?" I asked.

"It's a long story," he said as if he really wasn't ready to share it with us.

"We have a long time," I said flatly.

Travis looked from me to Monica, then back to me. I was sure that his mind was going a mile a minute in an effort to decide if he was going to tell us the whole story, or what part of his story he would tell us.

"I might as well tell you everything. You'll probably find out soon enough anyway," he said, the tone of his voice showing that it was time.

"I first met Robin a little over eighteen months ago. She was visiting an old lady in the hospital that was in the bed next to my sister."

"I didn't know you had a sister."

"Well, I do," he said rather sharply with a hint of anger in his voice.

"What was she in the hospital for?" Monica asked softly.

"She was in the hospital for treatment of cancer. She has been in and out of the hospital a number of times in the past two years. You can check that out, McCord," he said as he glared at me.

"What about you and Robin?" I asked.

"Like I said, I met her in the hospital. At first we started going to the hospital café for coffee, then later for lunch from time to time. After awhile, I asked her out to dinner. We met several times at the hospital. We would go out for something to eat at a nearby restaurant after we finished our visits at the hospital.

"We grew close over the weeks. Eventually, we became lovers. It was after we became lovers that I gave her the pin."

"Did you know that she was Tony Angelini's girl?"

"Not until we were pretty deeply involved. By then, it didn't matter. Robin said that she was going to tell Tony that it was over between them, and that she could not go with a man who used cocaine. Tony was pretty rough on her when he was high."

"What about you," I asked. "Did Robin know about your past?"

"Yes. Well, not at first. I told her everything about my past when it became clear to me that I was falling in love with her. She said it didn't matter as long I would not be like that any more."

"Did she believe you?"

"Yes," he replied sharply. "You can check my records. I haven't even received a traffic ticket since I met her, but I'd gladly change that if I could find out who killed her."

The expression on his face convinced me that he was telling the truth. I don't know why I believed him, but I did. It might have been because his police record supported his story, or maybe it was because I wanted to believe him.

"I loved her, McCord. She was the only woman for me. We were going to leave here and start a new life somewhere far away from here. Somewhere where Tony couldn't bother us."

"When was Robin going to tell Tony that it was over between them?" I asked.

"The night before she was found dead on the beach," he replied, his voice filled with sadness.

"Did you know it was Robin that Jonathan Ehman found on the beach that afternoon when you were in the park?"

"No. Not until I heard it on the news. All I knew was that a body had been found. I was questioned by a police officer and let go."

"You never did answer my earlier question as to why you were in the park that day. Why were you?"

"I told you, I got a call to go to the park between one and two in the afternoon."

"Who called you?"

"Bob Wray. He called me and said that Lieutenant Brooks wanted to see me in the park."

"So you went at Brooks's request?"

"Yes. I owed Lieutenant Brooks for getting me out of a couple of jams in the past. He had been hitting on me to do a couple of jobs for him, but I told him that I was out of the business. I told him that all I wanted was to be left alone and to work in my uncle's jewelry store."

"I take it he wasn't going to take no for an answer."

"Right. I wasn't going to go, but I decided to go to get him off my back, once and for all."

"Did you plan to kill him?"

"No, of course not. I was going to tell him to leave me alone or I would go to the cops with everything I knew about him.

"I worked for Tony off and on for several years. That is up until my sister got ill and I met Robin. I also did a few little jobs for Brooks."

"What kind of jobs?"

He let out a sigh and looked down at the floor. It was clear to me that he was trying to decide if he should tell me.

"I guess it doesn't matter if I go to jail or not. I'll tell you if you will get the person who murdered Robin."

"I'll get the person who murdered Robin whether you tell me or not," I assured him.

He sighed then went on.

"I bought a few drugs and did a little muscle work for Tony Angelini. There was a guy who tried to welsh on a drug deal with Tony. Brooks had me work the guy over. When I got arrested for it, Brooks made sure that it never went to trial. I did things like that. Each time, Brooks would make sure that it never went to trial. The one time that it did go to trial, Brooks made sure there were no witnesses at the trial."

"So Brooks was Tony's inside man in the police department."

"Right."

"Who gave you your instructions on who and when to muscle them? Was it Brooks or Tony?"

"I took my orders from Brooks, but they came from Tony."

"Are you sure?" I asked thoughtfully.

"Yes, I'm sure. Tony wanted no connection between him and the guy he wanted someone to work over. Brooks used Mitken, Charley Mitken, on occasion. I may have taken my orders from Brooks, but Tony was behind it."

"If I can keep you out of jail, will you help me put Brooks and Tony away?" I asked.

I could see that he was thinking about what I had asked. I glanced over at Monica.

"Travis, how is your sister doing?" Monica asked.

He looked at her a moment before answering.

"Not well. I think it would kill her if I went to jail, not that she will live much longer anyway."

"I'm sure that she would not want you to return to a life of crime. And I'm sure Robin would not want you to, either," Monica said softly. "Help us, and we'll help you."

He looked from her to me, then back to her.

"Okay. I'll help you put Tony and Brooks away, if you will keep me out of jail until after my sister dies. After that, I don't care."

Monica looked at me. I could tell by the look on her face that she was hoping that I would agree to his request.

"I can't make any promises, but I will do everything I can to keep you out of jail as long as you work with me."

"That's fair enough. I know your reputation. What do I do now?"

"Take the jewelry from the chest that belongs to you and get out of here. Don't come back here again. Go out the back way and go back to work as if nothing has changed," I instructed him.

Travis looked at me as if he was trying to believe what I said.

"When you get back home, I want you to write down dates, times, people, anything you can remember about where Brooks or Tony told you to hit on someone. I want every detail you can remember. I'll be in touch with you when I'm ready to drop the hammer on Brooks."

He nodded his head that he understood, then knelt down in front of the jewelry chest. He took out several pieces of jewelry, leaving three very expensive pieces behind.

"What about those?" I asked.

"They're not mine," he replied as he glanced down at them.

"Do you know who they might belong to?"

"Robin," he replied as he looked back at me.

"Do you know who gave them to her?"

"That necklace, the one with the sapphire surrounded by diamonds, I know was given to her by Tony Angelini."

"How do you know that?"

"He bought it in my uncle's store about a year or so ago."

I nodded that I understood. As he turned and left the apartment, I sat down on the bed to think. Monica came over and sat down beside me.

"Do you believe him?" she asked.

"Yes. At this point, he has nothing more to lose. He'll lose his sister before long. He has already lost the one woman he loved."

"What do we do now?"

"I think it's time to get out of here."

"What about the jewelry?"

"Leave it. We know what's left. I got a feeling that someone will be coming here to get the rest of it."

"Who?"

"I think Tony will send Brooks to get it."

"Why? If they didn't find it before, what makes you think they will find it now?"

"Because we're going to leave the drawer open a little. It has to look like it popped open when it was moved."

"You are sneaky. Are we going to keep an eye on this place?"

"No. We're going to let Wray tell us when they have found the jewelry."

"And just how are you going to do that?"

"When he quits watching the place, we'll know that Tony got what he wanted from here, namely the jewelry. Now, let's get out of here."

I stood up and reached out to Monica. She took my hand as I helped her to her feet. I let go of her hand and knelt down in front of the chest. After closing the drawer, I pulled it open just enough so someone searching the room would see it.

I got up and followed Monica to the door. I opened the door just a crack to make sure that no one was in the hall. The hall was clear.

We left the apartment building by the back door and went down the alley. We returned to my car in the parking lot, got in and drove back to my apartment.

CHAPTER SEVENTEEN

It was still sprinkling when we arrived back at my apartment shortly after one in the afternoon. As I pulled into the parking lot, I noticed a large black Cadillac parked next to the curb. There was no doubt in my mind that Frank Angelini was in the car and that he was waiting to see me.

"Looks like we have company," I said as I drove into the garage and shut off the engine.

"The black Cadillac?"

"Yeah. That's Frank Angelini's car."

"You think he's waiting in your apartment?"

"No. Frank's too arrogant for that. He would expect me to come to him. He's in the car."

"What are you going to do?"

"Go talk to him. I want you to wait here."

I got out of the car and walked out to the curb. As I approached the car, the rear door opened. I bent down and looked inside.

"Hello, Frank. What brings you to my neck of the woods?"

"Get in out of the rain."

"Sorry. I have a lady friend waiting for me."

"This won't take but a minute."

"You can wait until I escort my lady friend to my apartment. If not, then too bad."

I had no intentions of letting Frank think that he was in charge for even one minute. He was going to have to play by my rules this time if he wanted to talk to me. Frank hesitated as he looked at me, then gave a single nod. I turned around and walked back to the garage. As I approached my car, Monica got out.

"What does he want?"

"I don't know, but he says he wants to talk."

"What did you tell him?"

"I told him I was going to escort you up to my apartment first. If he wanted to talk to me, he was going to have to wait until I come back down."

"You be careful around him. I don't trust him."

"I don't trust him, either," I said as I slipped the key into the trunk lock of my car.

I opened the trunk, moved a blanket off a small metal box, then unlocked the box. Inside the box was a 9mm pistol. Keeping my back towards Frank's car so he could not see what I was doing, I checked the gun to make sure it was loaded and ready to use. I then slipped it in my belt, under my coat. I took Monica by the arm and led her to my apartment.

Monica hadn't said anything about the gun. She already knew what kind of people I had to deal with and had said earlier that she understood the need for a gun at times.

Just as we entered the apartment building, I glanced back over my shoulder. Frank had closed the car door, but rolled down a window so he could watch us. I wondered what he was thinking as we climbed the three flights of steps to my apartment.

Once I had Monica safely inside my apartment, I went back downstairs. The door to Frank's car opened as I approached it. I climbed in and sat down next to Frank.

"Well, Frank, what's so important?"

"Let's go for a little ride," Frank said as Joe Martonie started the car.

"Let's not. Shut off the engine, Joe," I said.

Frank looked at me as if he was thinking about telling Joe to drive, but seemed to change his mind.

"Do as he says, Joe," Frank relented.

"Joe, take a walk," I said.

Joe turned and looked at me, then at his boss. I wasn't sure what he was going to do, but I knew he would not do anything without Frank telling him.

Frank sat for several seconds just looking at me. Suddenly, he turned toward Joe.

"Do as he says."

"But boss....."

"Do as he says, Joe," Frank insisted.

I waited until Joe was out of the car and had walked several yards down the sidewalk. I watched him as he turned around and stood looking at the car. I knew he could not see us through the dark tinted glass windows, but I could see him.

"Okay, Frank. What do you want?"

"I want to know if you have found out who killed Robin?"

"I have a pretty good idea who did it. I even think I know why. I'm also pretty sure who it was that tried to cover it up."

"Tell me?" he asked excitedly.

"I don't think you want to hear who killed Robin," I said as I watched him for some kind of reaction.

"You think my son killed her, don't you? You think that my son gave her an overdose of drugs, then shot her in the back of the head."

"I know what killed her. I just can't prove who did it. I can assure you that as soon as I can, I'll have him behind bars."

Frank looked at me as if he was sizing me up. I was wondering how he had gotten that much information, it had not been on the news. Brooks certainly wouldn't have told him, he worked for Tony. Brooks was not so stupid that he would cancel his meal ticket by telling Frank anything.

I also wondered what was going through Frank's mind, and why he didn't come to his only son's defense. Was it possible that he already knew that his son had killed Robin, or was it because he wasn't sure and was hoping that I would find out that someone else did it?

"You won't be arresting anyone, McCord," Frank said, the look in his eyes showing how angry he was with me.

"You've been suspended from the police department for killing a man. You're not a cop any more. If you don't help me find out who killed Robin, I'll see to it that you never wear a badge again."

"I wouldn't put money on it, if I were you," I said as I reached back and opened the door.

I didn't take my eyes off him as I backed out of the car. The look on his face gave me a clue as to how angry he was with me. I think the only thing that was keeping him from having Joe work me over, was the lack of privacy. It could cause him a lot of trouble if he were to have Joe try to work me over in such a public place, to say nothing of the fact that I would not hesitate to shoot Joe if he tried.

"I think Mr. Angelini is ready to go home, Joe," I said as I quickly glanced toward Martonie.

Joe looked from me to his boss, then back at me. He looked like he wasn't sure what to do.

"Joe, be a good boy and get him out of here before I really get upset," I said as I slipped my hand under my coat.

Joe looked at my coat where I rested my hand, then walked toward the car. He never took his eyes off me as he got in behind the wheel and started the car. I noticed that he looked over his shoulder at Frank before he put the car into gear and drove away.

I let out a sigh of relief as I watched the car turn the corner and disappear from sight. I was sure that it would not be over between us, but right now I had other things to think about. Namely, getting myself out of hot water.

As I started to turn around to go back to my apartment, I noticed a car parked across the street in the bank parking lot. It sort of caught my eye because I was not used to seeing cars parked at the bank when it was closed. I also noticed that there were two men sitting in it. From the looks of the car, it was probably the police watching my apartment. I wondered how long they had been watching me. They had probably been there since early this morning when I "left town" with Monica. There was no doubt in my mind that they had already reported the fact that I was back and that Monica was still with me.

I smiled to myself, then waved at them before turning and walking back into the apartment building. When I reached the third floor landing, I found Monica waiting for me. I could see the worry in her eyes.

"What happened," she asked before I could get in the door.

I guided her back into the apartment and closed the door.

"There are too many ears around here."

She stood in front of me looking up at me. She was waiting for an answer. I took her hand and led her to the sofa where we sat down.

I told her what had happened, and that Frank Angelini was very upset with me. We talked about the past few days and tried to put things in perspective. Although we had eliminated a number of suspects in the murder of Robin, we still had nothing that we could prove.

As I tipped my head back and looked up at the ceiling, I let out a long sigh. My mind could no longer think clearly. There were just too many unanswered questions.

"I have an idea," Monica said. "Why don't we get something to eat? We haven't eaten since this morning."

"I am not very hungry."

"I think we should relax and try to forget about everything until we've had a chance to rest. Try to put it out of our minds until tomorrow. Maybe, we will be able to think better then."

"I don't know if I can do that, I mean shut off my mind like that," I said as I looked at her.

"I don't want you to shut off your mind. I just want you to direct your thinking in another direction. I think I can help you with that," she said as she leaned close to me and kissed me lightly on the lips.

I quickly found that it was easier than I thought to forget about the case and think about her. As soon as she backed away and looked at me with that special smile of hers, I found that I was feeling a little hungry after all.

"Maybe I can eat something," I said with a smile.

I stood up and helped her to her feet. As I took her in my arms, I heard the crash of thunder. I suddenly realized that it had started to rain hard again. Arm in arm we walked out to the kitchen where we prepared dinner together.

After a good meal, we cleaned up the kitchen, then went back into the living room. We sat down on the sofa together. I reached over and picked up the television remote.

"I'd rather not watch television right now," she said softly. "Can't we just sit and listen to the rain and thunder?"

"Sure, but I know of a better place to do that."

"Where?" she asked with a smile.

"In my bed."

"I like that idea. Will you give me a couple of minutes?"

"Sure. Just call me when you're ready."

Monica gave me a light kiss on the cheek, then stood up. I watched her as she left the room. She was one very sexy lady.

I leaned back and relaxed as I waited for her to call me. I remembered the first time I saw her was on the front porch of a lodge in northern Wisconsin. It had been a cool rainy evening much like this one.

My thoughts of her were disturbed when I heard the door to my bedroom open. I looked up and saw her standing there, leaning against the doorframe in just a towel. God, she looked so sexy as she smiled at me. I would have no trouble forgetting about the case this evening, I was sure of that.

"Why don't you shut off the lights and come to bed?" she whispered, then turned around and disappeared into the bedroom.

I didn't waste a minute. I locked the door, shut off the lights and went into the bedroom. When the lightning flashed, I could see her climbing into bed. The towel was gone. Her naked body glowed in the brief flash of light. I could not seem to get my clothes off fast enough so I could join her in bed.

Leaving my clothes in a heap on the floor, I climbed into bed beside her. She rolled up against me. We were soon wrapped in each other's arms, and in our love for each other. The sound of the rain against the window and the sounds of thunder were no longer heard. We spent the rest of the day in bed making love and enjoying each other's company.

I don't know what time it was when we finally drifted off to sleep, but it really didn't matter. She had made me forget my troubles for a little while, at least long enough for me to get some much needed rest.

* * * *

It was very early in the morning when I woke. Monica was curled up against me, her warm body reminding me of the love we had shared. The feel of her soft skin under my hands as I lightly touched her back and shoulders made me think of her, and of us.

What was I doing here with this beautiful woman? What did we have in common? I could not think of anything except that we loved each other. She was smart, well educated, beautiful, loving and sexy. She was everything any man could want in a woman. I was just a city cop with little to offer a woman like her. Yet, here she was, sleeping at my side.

As I lay on my back looking up at the ceiling, I began to let my thoughts drift off into space. Even with this beautiful woman lying beside me, her leg curled over mine and her arm resting across my chest, I could not keep from thinking about who had killed Robin. She had been a very lovely girl who had her whole life in front of her.

Limiting my thoughts to just Tony left my mind with room to think, to take one thing at a time and carefully pick it apart. Right now, it was Tony Angelini. I mentally reviewed what I had learned about him. He was tall, dark and handsome, and he had money. He was also a drug pusher and drug user, and he didn't hesitate to use whatever method was needed to get what he wanted, including the use of brutality. He was a very jealous man, jealous to the point of violence. Had it been this jealousy that had caused him to killed Robin, or was it something else? Or did someone else murder her?

As I tried to think of a reason, I remembered two very important things. The first was the letter that Robin had planned to send to Tony's father. The letter alone might not have been enough of a reason to cause Tony to kill her. But add to that the fact that Robin had a lover, assuming that she had told Tony about it, there was certainly ample cause for a jealous man like Tony to go crazy enough to kill her.

But then there was the question of why kill her twice? Why would he inject her with enough cocaine to kill her almost immediately, and then shoot her in the back of the head? It didn't make sense. And where was the gun that had killed her?

I mulled over each question in my mind as I lay looking up at the dark ceiling. I tried to come up with something that would resemble logical answers. I couldn't picture Tony doing it alone. He may have given her the overdose of cocaine in a rage, but I doubted he would have shot her, too. I came to the conclusion that there had to be at least two people involved in her death.

As I thought about it, I remembered the way that Frank Angelini had talked to me in his car just hours earlier. He never once tried to defend his son. If he believed that his son had killed Robin, then it was just as likely that he knew his son was a drug user. The question still remained as to how would he have found out that Robin had been drugged and shot? Brooks would not want him to find that out.

Then it came to me. The package that Wray handed over to the unknown man in the café must have found its way to Frank. Wray was not stupid. He would not give something like that to a stranger, and Frank wouldn't take the chance of being seen taking it. Therefore, it only seemed logical that the man in the café had to be the only man that Frank Angelini would trust completely with such a package, Joe Martonie. That would explain how Frank got inside information on the investigation, inside information that Brooks would not want him to have.

It also made me wonder who Wray was really working for. If he was giving that kind of information to Frank, then he was double-crossing Brooks. That thought caused me to smile. If Brooks ever found out that Wray was double-crossing him, he would eliminate Wray in a heartbeat.

My thoughts drifted back to my other suspects. First, there was Lieutenant Brooks. He had already proven to me that he was a cold-blooded killer. He was also very clever. After all, he had set me up to take the fall for Mitken's murder. Brooks had managed to get me off the case and leak to the news just the information that he wanted them to have. He had planted so many suspects in the park that it made it difficult to figure out what was going on, and who was really involved.

The more I thought about it, the more I began to understand Brooks. The more I thought about Brooks, the more I was convinced that he had killed Robin. If nothing else, he had made the effort to cover it up to protect Tony. If I was going to solve this case and get myself out of trouble, I was going to have to prove that Brooks and Tony were the killers; or that one of them killed her, and the other was an accomplice.

Monica suddenly interrupted my thoughts as she moved against me. She slid her hand across my chest then she rose up and looked at me.

"You okay?" she asked softly.

"I'm fine," I replied, but I don't think she believed me.

"I know you're worried, but things will work out."

"I know."

I may have said that I knew things would work out, but I wasn't convinced. All the evidence the police had on Mitken's murder pointed right at me. Unless I could prove that I didn't kill Mitken, I would lose everything that meant anything to me. I would lose my job, my reputation as an honest cop, but most of all I would lose Monica.

"I'm going to take a shower. When I'm done, I'll fix us breakfast. I know you think better on a full stomach. Then we can sit down and figure out what we need to do to get this all cleared up," she said with her usual tone of optimism.

I wanted to believe her more than anything in the world. I reached up and pulled her down over me until our lips met. The warmth of her breasts against my chest, the feel of her hand on my side, and the feel of her back as I lightly ran my hand over her, gave me a renewed hope that maybe she was right. Maybe things would work out for us.

After a long, deep kiss, she rose up and smiled down at me. I could see the sparkle in her beautiful eyes.

"I love you. I'm not going to let anything happen to you," she said softly.

I smiled up at her, then watched her roll away from me. I could not take my eyes off her as she walked around the bed and disappeared into the bathroom. I closed my eyes and let my mind think of her as I heard the water running in the shower. She was the only woman I had ever met that could make me believe that she could actually make everything all right.

CHAPTER EIGHTEEN

When I came out of the bathroom after a long warm shower, I could hear Monica in the kitchen fixing breakfast. I began to think about her and what was ahead for us. She would go back to Madison to her job in the history department. I would return to my job, or would I?

The sudden thought that I might not have a job to go back to, brought me back to a realization that I was not ready to face. I knew I was innocent, but the evidence sure didn't prove it. Unless things took a turn for the better, I might very well end up in jail along with those that I had sent there.

I finished dressing and went out to the kitchen. Monica was wearing the robe that caressed her figure. She looked so lovely this morning that I could not stand to just look at her. The thought that I might lose her, if I could not prove my innocence, made me want to hold onto her.

I stepped up in front of her and took her in my arms. She wrapped her arms around my neck and held onto me. I buried my face in her soft hair at her neck and smelled the light fragrance of it. As she pressed against me and held me tightly, I could sense the urgency in her.

I reluctantly let go of her and looked down into her cobalt blue eyes. I could see a tear in the corner of her eye. We both seemed to know that it would not be long before I would be arrested for the murder of Charlie Mitken. Facing that would be hard for both of us.

I could not stand to see her cry, nor could I stand to see her dragged into this mess. The press would be all over this like a pack of hyenas fighting over a meal. It would be best for her to distance herself from me as much as possible. If the news media got hold of the fact that we were lovers, and that she was Doctor Barnhart of the University of Wisconsin, her career could be ruined, too.

"I think you should go back to Madison. I don't want you here when they arrest me," I said as I looked at her face.

"I can't leave you when you need me the most," she protested.

"But your career?"

"My career? What's my career got to do with us? We're together and we'll stick together until we prove you didn't kill Mitken, And we will prove it if it takes forever," she said with determination.

I looked into her eyes. What I saw there convinced me that together we might find a way to prove that I didn't kill Mitken.

"You want to really help me?" I asked.

"Yes, but not by returning to Madison," she added stubbornly.

"Good. Let's have breakfast and figure out how we are going to get Brooks to confess to the killing of Mitken or at least get someone to point a finger at him," I said, putting as much confidence in my voice as I could muster.

Monica smiled and gave me a hug and a kiss before we settled down to making and eating breakfast. While we ate, we discussed ways that we might be able to get Brooks to confess. Over the next couple of hours we came up with a plan. There was no doubt that it would be risky, but it could work.

The only real problem I could see with our plan was to get Captain Sinclair to go along with it. The time had come for me to trust him, to believe that he was the kind of a cop I thought him to be. I would be stretching my luck and our years of friendship to expect him to stick his neck out for me, but I didn't see that I had a choice.

I made a call to Captain Sinclair at his home and asked him to meet us at the station. I gave him a brief rundown on what we had in mind and asked him to help us. He agreed to help, but reminded me it was risky at best. I had no problem agreeing with him.

We got dressed and went out to my car. As I opened the garage door, I glanced across the street toward the bank. There in the parking lot was a plain looking car with two men sitting in it.

"They're still there," I commented.

"I know. I saw them," Monica said as she got in the car.

I got in, started the car and backed out of the garage, then drove out onto the street. A quick glance in the rearview mirror revealed that the plain car was following me about half a block back.

They stayed back at a good distance until I turned into the police garage. Instead of following us into the garage, they drove past and parked down the street. It crossed my mind that they might have a very long wait.

After parking, I led Monica to Captain Sinclair's office. Captain Sinclair was waiting for us. He immediately motioned for us to come into his office. I held the door for Monica, then followed her into his office. He was on the phone, so we sat down and waited for him to finish his call.

"I'll see you shortly," he said, then hung up the phone and turned toward me.

"This had better work, Nick. Lieutenant Brooks is on his way over here. He thinks we are about to hang you out to dry."

"I sure hope it doesn't work out that way," I commented.

"I take it that this is your expert on jewelry?" Captain Sinclair said as he stood up and held out his hand.

"Yes, sir. Captain, this is Doctor Monica Barnhart of the University of Wisconsin History Department. Monica, this is Captain Joe Sinclair."

"Nice to meet you, Captain Sinclair."

"Nice to meet you, Doctor."

"Please, call me Monica."

"Well, Monica, what has Nick dragged you into?"

"Nothing. I more or less went willingly," she said with a smile.

Captain Sinclair smiled, then looked over at me. As he looked at me, his smile sort of faded away. I wasn't sure just what was going to happen from here.

"Okay, Nick. I stuck my neck way out for you this time. I have everyone you asked for either being picked up by trusted officers or coming in under my orders."

"Thank you, sir."

"I sure hope this works."

"So do we," Monica replied.

"How do you want to play this out?"

"I would like to make sure that Lieutenant Brooks sees everyone that we have called in, but I don't want him left for even a second where he can talk to them. I want him to be nervous from the very start," I explained.

"Okay, that's easy enough. We can have everyone sitting in the hall. He'll have to walk past every one of them."

"Good."

"What are you hoping for?"

"I'm hoping that at least one of them, Brooks or Tony, will break and tell us something that will lead us to the truth."

"What truth are we looking for?" Captain Sinclair asked.

"The one that proves that Brooks killed Charley Mitken, and the one that leads us to the killer, or killers, of Robin Flower."

"I can go along with that. Just how would you like to handle this?"

"I would like you to be with Lieutenant Brooks at all times. I want him to be in the viewing room with you while the others are questioned. I want him to see and hear everything. Keep a close eye on him. I'm hoping that what some of the others say about him will make him talk."

"That's not going to be easy. He's an experienced cop. He knows how these things are done," Captain Sinclair warned.

"I know, but I'm counting on one of the others pinning him with enough that he comes unglued and says something stupid by mistake. One thing I have learned about Brooks is that he has a bit of a temper. I'm hoping it will be his downfall."

"I think he's crazy," Captain Sinclair said as he looked at Monica.

"I know, but that's what I like about him," she replied with a smile.

"Okay, when do we start?" Captain Sinclair asked.

"As soon as we get Ehman and Lieutenant Brooks here."

"Brooks should be here in about twenty minutes. Ehman was picked up just before you got here and is being brought in. He should be here before Brooks."

"What about the others?"

"Most of them are already here and waiting in the hall outside the interrogation room. Where are you going to be?"

"I'm going to question Ehman, Fox, Martonie, and Tony Angelini with Bill Martin. If we don't get any results, then you and Martin will question me about the death of Mitken."

"You better act like your life depends on getting to the bottom of Robin's death," Captain Sinclair reminded me.

"Don't worry. I think it does. I think Mitken knew who killed Robin, that's why he was killed. And I think they tried to pin his murder on me because I was getting too close and they needed to discredit me. They wanted me out of the way, but they knew that it would cause too many problems if they out and out killed me."

"Okay, then let's get at it. Who do you want first?"

"Let's start with Joe Martonie. Put him in the room and when you're ready, call me in from the viewing room next door. I want Brooks to hear all of this, every single word."

"What about me?" Monica asked. "I can't very well be in the viewing room with Brooks, and I certainly can't be in the interrogation room."

"You can be in the viewing room on the other side. From there we can pipe in what is said from the interrogation room and from the viewing room where Brooks will be. There will be an officer in that room with you. He will be recording everything that's said in the other two rooms."

Monica nodded that she understood. We left Sinclair's office and went to our places to act out what I hoped would be the final curtain for Brooks and Tony. Monica went into the one room so that she would not be seen by any of the suspects while I waited in Sinclair's office for him to call.

It took awhile for Brooks to arrive. I sat alone thinking of all the things that could go wrong with our plan and what would happen if it failed.

Finally, everyone was in place and I was called. I went into the interrogation room where I found Sergeant Bill Martin leaning against the wall. Joe Martonie was sitting at the table. I acknowledged Martin's presence with a nod, but went right to work on Joe.

"Hello, Joe. How are you doing?"

"I'm fine," he replied cautiously.

"Are you a little nervous?"

"A little."

"That's all right. This won't take long."

"I thought you were done talking to me."

"I have just a few questions I want to ask you, and a few things I want to get clear in my mind. Is that okay?"

"Mr. Angelini said I didn't have to talk to you or the police without a lawyer unless I wanted to."

"That's right, Joe. Do you want a lawyer?"

"Am I a suspect?"

"Not really. I don't think you did anything. I don't plan to lock you up, if that's what you're worried about," I assured him.

"Okay, but if I decide I want a lawyer later, will that be okay?"

"Sure, Joe. Anytime you decide that you want a lawyer, we'll stop questioning you until your lawyer gets here. Okay?"

"Okay," he said after he considered what I had said. "What do you want to know?"

"Joe, how did you feel about Robin Flower?"

"She was nice. She would talk to me when no one else would. I liked her," he said, the tone of his voice indicating that he really did like Robin.

"Did you ever have a chance to talk with her alone?"

"You mean, just the two of us, with no one else around?"

"Yes, Joe."

"A couple of times, I guess," he said softly as if it hurt for him to think about it.

"Tell me about the last time you were alone with Robin?"

"There was this party at Mr. Angelini's house."

"You mean, Frank Angelini's?"

"Yeah. Well, it was getting pretty dull and I was feeling kind of down. I was the only one who didn't have a partner that evening. I guess Miss Flower was feeling sorry for me or something, 'cause she asked me to take a walk with her."

"Where did you go?"

"We walked out to the garden and sat down on a stone bench near the pool. We must have been there for an hour, maybe more. We was just talking, honest."

"I believe you. What were you talking about?"

"At first, we talked about me. You know, things like how I was getting along without my wife, how was everyone treating me, that sort of thing. Later, we began to talk about her."

"What did she tell you about herself?"

"She said that she didn't love Tony any more. She said that he was still using drugs and that she didn't like that. She said that he hit her once after she said something to another man.

"She told me that she had found a new guy, but she wouldn't tell me his name. She also told me that she was going to tell Mr. Angelini, Frank, that Tony was using drugs. I warned her not to do that. I told her that Tony had a mean temper, but she already knew that. I told her that he would hurt her if she tried to leave him or tell his father about the drugs."

Joe stopped talking and looked down at his hands. I was sure that I could see a tear in the corner of his eye. There was no doubt in my mind that he was sure that Tony had killed Robin, but there was some doubt in my mind that Tony had done it by himself.

"When was this party, Joe?"

"It was the night before her body was found in the park."

"You said you were called to show up in the park. Who called you?"

"I'm not sure, but I've been giving it some thought since you talked to me at Mr. Angelini's house. I think it was Bob Wray," he said.

"Do you know Bob Wray?"

"Sure. He's been to Mr. Angelini's house several times."

"In fact, you received a large yellow envelope from Wray in a little café only a few blocks from this police station, didn't you?"

The look on Joe's face told me that he had been sure that no one had seen him, but now he knew better.

"Yes," he admitted reluctantly.

"What was in the envelope?"

"I don't know."

"You don't know?"

"That's what I said, I don't know."

Joe seemed to be getting a little agitated. I didn't want to push him too hard and have him ask for a lawyer. The delay might cause my plan to fall apart.

"Okay, Joe. I believe you. Can you tell me this, what did you do with the envelope?"

"I don't think I should tell you."

"Why not?"

"I don't think Mr. Angelini would like it."

"Frank or Tony, Joe?"

"Frank," he said, then suddenly realized that he had answered my question.

"You tricked me. I'm not talking to you any more without a lawyer," he said as he crossed his arms in front his chest and pressed his lips firmly together.

"That's all right, Joe. I don't think I have any more questions for you, anyway."

He looked at me with a look of surprise. He then looked at Martin, who was still leaning against the wall next to the door.

"You can go, Joe," Martin said.

Joe stood up, looked at both of us, then turned to leave. When he reached the door, he turned back and looked at me.

"I hope you find out who killed Miss Flower."

"Joe, is Wray working for Tony or for Frank?"

Joe stared at me for what seemed to be a very long time. The look on his face made me think that he was trying to decide if he should answer me or not.

"He works for Frank," he said, then turned and walked out the door.

I looked over at Martin. I knew Sinclair was behind the mirror with Brooks. I was wondering what was going through Brooks' mind at this moment. He had to be really angry. Here all this time he thought Wray was his snitch when the truth was he was working for Frank.

"Well, what do you think?" Martin asked.

"I think he doesn't know very much, but he did establish that Tony has a mean temper and that he gets very jealous about who talks to his girlfriend."

"That still doesn't prove anything," Martin said, disappointment showing on his face.

"You're right about that. I think it's time to talk to Travis Fox. Go get him, please."

Martin nodded then stepped out of the room. Within a few minutes, he returned with Travis. He pointed to the seat and Travis sat down. I sat down across the table from him.

"Mr. Fox, you understand why you're here, don't you?"

"Sure."

"For the record, you've been read your rights?"

"Sure. I don't need a lawyer for what I have to say."

"In that case, I want you to tell me about your relationship with Robin Flower."

"We were lovers," he replied calmly.

"Did you know that she was involved with Tony Angelini?"

"Not at first, but by the time I found out it didn't matter. We were in love."

"When was that?"

"Almost six months ago."

"How serious had you become?"

"We planned to go away together. Somewhere where Tony's temper wouldn't be a problem."

"When was the last time you saw Robin?"

"I saw her a couple of days before she was found on the beach."

"What did you talk about that day?"

"We talked about the same things we always talked about, leaving Wisconsin and having a life together."

"There was more to it than that, wasn't there?"

"Yes," he admitted. "She said she was going to a party at Frank Angelini's place, and that she planned to tell Frank that Tony was using drugs and that she no longer loved his son. She was also going to tell him that she was leaving town and would not be returning."

"Do you know if she told Frank Angelini that, or not?"

"No. Not for sure. I never got another chance to talk to her."

"Was she going to call you after the party?"

"No. We had planned to meet at the hospital on the day her body was found," he said, his voice choking on the words.

"Someone told you to go to the park that day. Why did you go to the park if you were planning on meeting Robin at the hospital?"

"I wasn't supposed to meet Robin until that evening. Tony was supposed to have some kind of a meeting at his warehouse that night and she would be free to see me."

"Who told you to be at the park that afternoon?"

"Lieutenant John Brooks," he replied.

"Why would Lieutenant Brooks want you to go to the park?"

"I guessed that it was really Tony that wanted to see me in the park. You see, Brooks is one of Tony's hired hands. Tony would never contact me directly, he was too much like his dad in that respect. He would expect me to come anytime he called me."

"Why would Tony think that? Didn't you have a falling out with him around the time you decided that you would have nothing more to do with him?"

"Yeah, but I figured if Robin had told him that I was her lover, he would want to see me personally."

"Wasn't that asking for a confrontation?"

"Maybe, but the one thing Robin didn't understand about Tony was that he would not let us have a moment's peace if I didn't assure him that his life was not worth a nickel if he got in our way."

"So you went there planning to confront him, even threaten him?"

"Yeah, more or less."

"Did you see him anywhere around the park?" I asked.

"No. I did see Lieutenant Brooks, but I wasn't interested in talking to him. I was looking for Tony."

"How long was Brooks hanging around the park?"

"I don't know, but he was there when I got there."

"How long were you in the park?"

"A little over two hours before I was stopped and questioned by a police officer about the body found on the beach. I didn't know it was Robin until late the next day when I heard it on the news."

"If you were in the park for over two hours, why didn't you go talk to Brooks if you knew he was one of Tony's "hired hands", as you put it?"

"I didn't want to talk to him. I figured if he wanted to talk to me, he would have come to me. He knew I was there."

"He'd been watching you?"

"Not all the time, but he had seen me."

"What did you do when Robin failed to show up at the hospital?"

"After I visited my sister at the hospital, I tried to call Robin at her apartment. I didn't get an answer. I figured that she might need some time alone, so I decided to wait until the next day to go see her. I found out about her on the news before I had a chance to go to her apartment."

I could tell that Travis was having a hard time dealing with the questions about Robin. I was sure that he had nothing to do with Robin's death. I was hoping that what he had said about Lieutenant Brooks was sinking into Captain Sinclair's mind and eating at Brooks.

I looked over at Martin to see if he had any questions that he wanted answered. He shook his head indicating that he had no questions of this man.

"I guess you can go. If I have anything further, I'll give you a call," I said as I leaned back in my chair.

I waited for Travis to leave before I left the interrogation room. I was getting impatient and needed to take a break. I also needed to find out if Brooks had given any hint of his involvement in the death of Robin.

As I stepped out into the hall, I saw Captain Sinclair direct Lieutenant Brooks to go with another officer. I wasn't sure if he had been placed under arrest or not, but he was at least being detained.

Captain Sinclair motioned for me to join him in his office. I nodded in response, then looked over my shoulder to see Monica come out of the other room. She quickly joined me, then walked with me to Captain Sinclair's office.

CHAPTER NINETEEN

I followed Monica into Captain Sinclair's office. As she sat down on the sofa, I sat beside her. I wasn't sure what was going on, but from the look on Sinclair's face, it didn't look good. I waited until he sat down behind his desk before saying anything.

"Are we making any headway?"

"Not much, Nick. All we've done so far is to piss Brooks off. You've managed to indicate that he might be a crooked cop and that he might have inside connections with one of Milwaukee's crime boss families. But so far there isn't any proof. We need proof," Captain Sinclair insisted. "If we continue like we have been, you may well be burying yourself."

"I don't see that I have any other choice. Unless I can prove that Brooks was involved in the death of Robin, I won't be able to prove that he shot Mitken."

"Have you had any response at all from Brooks?" Monica asked.

"He looked a little nervous when Martonie talked about getting the envelope from Wray. I don't think he knew anything about it. The mention of Bob Wray made the veins in Brooks's neck stand out."

"Well, if that made his veins stand out, just think what will happen when I question Ehman."

"Wait, there's more. When Fox mentioned that Brooks told him to be in the park, Brooks just stood there looking at Fox through the glass. If looks could kill, Fox would have been dead. When Fox said that Brooks was, how did he put it - - ?"

"One of Tony's hired hands," I suggested.

"Yeah, that's it. Brooks said something under his breath that sounded like "you'll never prove that", then he looked at me. From the look on his face, I was sure that he was afraid that I heard his comment. I didn't say anything or indicate to him that I had heard him, but I did. If we're lucky, the recorder might have picked it up.

"The fact that Fox placed Brooks in the park over two hours before Robin's body was reported as found makes me tend to believe you. On the day the body was found, he said that he was driving by when the report came in. Unfortunately, what I believe, or don't believe, won't help you at your hearing."

"I think it's time to push him a little harder. Let's have a talk with Ehman. He should make Brooks really squirm."

"Okay, but Brooks is keeping his cool," Captain Sinclair replied as he stood up. "He's going to be a hard nut to crack."

Monica took hold of my arm and held me while Captain Sinclair left the room.

"Can I have a kiss," she asked looking up at me.

I smiled down at her and leaned toward her. As our lips met, I felt a warmth deep inside me. It was a warmth that made me more determined than ever to get Lieutenant Brooks behind bars for the murder of Charley Mitken, even if I couldn't get him for the murder of Robin Flower.

I looked into Monica's cobalt blue eyes and I could see the worry in them. I wanted to say something that would take away the worry, but at this moment there was nothing to say. We were still too far from getting me off the hook.

"I love you," I whispered.

She smiled up at me, squeezed my arm and gave me a wink. At that moment I wished that I had as much confidence that everything was going to turn out just fine, as she seemed to have. Frankly, I was scared to death.

"You go on ahead," she said.

I looked at her for a second before leaving her in Captain Sinclair's office. As I walked toward the interrogation room, I glanced back over my shoulder and saw her watching me. I couldn't swear to it, but I was almost sure that I could see the shine of a tear in her eye. It was impossible, of course, as I was too far away from her.

I knew that the next two people to be questioned were going to have to provide some very strong evidence pointing at Brooks, or I was in deep trouble. I would have to force myself in order to keep my concentration on the job at hand.

As I entered the interrogation room, I saw Sergeant Martin standing against the wall with his arms folded across his chest. He just stood there not saying a word. It had been his way all along, just standing there, listening while he waited for something to happen.

Sitting at the table was Jonathan Ehman. He looked a little nervous. I could see that he was wondering what was going to happen to him. I couldn't blame him for being a little nervous. Hell, I was.

"Hi, Jonathan. How you doing?"

"Okay, I guess."

"Do you understand why you're here?"

"To answer some questions?"

"That's right. What I want you to do is to go over the same things we talked about the other day. Is that okay?"

"Yeah, sure."

"Before we start, do you want a lawyer? You can have one if you want one."

"No. I'll talk to you."

"Good. Now, let's start with the basics. Do you know Lieutenant Brooks?"

"Sure."

"Tell me, for the record, how it is that you know him?"

"I first met Lieutenant Brooks when I got caught stealing electronics equipment from Mr. Angelini's warehouse."

"That's Tony Angelini's warehouse?"

"Yes."

"Did Brooks arrest you for that?"

"No. He questioned me about the missing equipment for a little while, but he seemed more interested in having me buy drugs for Mr. Angelini, Tony, from Danny Minger. He also said that he would not tell my mother about the stolen equipment if I would keep an eye on Tony for him."

"Did you agree to do that?"

"Yes."

"Go on," I said.

"Lieutenant Brooks wanted me to keep him informed on who came in and out of Tony's warehouse, what was done, how long they stayed. You know, things like that."

"Who were some of the people who came to the warehouse to meet with Tony?"

"There was Charley Mitken."

"What was he there for?"

"I don't know, but he had words with Tony a day or so before Robin was killed. He left looking really angry."

"Did you hear what the argument was about?"

"No. I couldn't understand much of what was being said. It sounded like Tony wanted Charley to pressure someone, I'm not sure who. It could have been a couple of Tony's drug dealers."

"Possibly, Danny Minger?"

"Could have been, but I can't say for sure."

"Who else came to the warehouse?"

"Joe Martonie came by the day before Robin died, too. Tony had some pretty ugly things to say to him. Tony accused Joe of flirting with Robin when he wasn't looking, but there was nothing between Joe and Robin. They might have been good friends if Tony wasn't so jealous of any man that talked to Robin."

"Did Travis Fox ever come to the warehouse?"

"Like I told you before, he came one time over a year ago. He was madder than hell. He told Tony if he ever dragged him into one of his dirty dealings again he would tell his father that he was using his own products. I never saw him after that."

"What can you tell me about Bob Wray?"

"Not very much. I overheard Lieutenant Brooks tell Tony that Wray had taken care of one of Tony's loose ends down at the jail and that he enjoyed doing it. The next day, I heard that Danny Minger died in jail while he was being held under protective custody."

"Did you see Lieutenant Brooks at the warehouse?"

"Sure. He would come in every few days. He used to meet with Tony in the office at least once a week, sometimes more often. Tony was paying Lieutenant Brooks to make sure that he was protected from the police."

"You mean that Brooks was working for Tony Angelini?"

"Yes."

"Do you know who killed Robin?"

"No."

"Okay, that'll be all for now. I want you to go back where you were. I'll be in touch with you later."

I sat at the table and watched as Jonathan left. Martin just stood there looking at me. I wondered what was going on behind the one-way glass.

"I think it's time to have a little talk with Wray."

"I'll get him," Martin said.

While I waited for Martin to return with Wray, I had a chance to think. So far, all I had accomplished was to show that Brooks might be a dirty cop. I had come no closer to proving anything. I had two more people to question after Wray, Tony and Brooks.

I looked up as Wray entered the interrogation room with Martin right behind him. The look on Wray's face told me he was angry that he had been dragged into this investigation.

"What the hell do you think you're doing, McCord?"

"I'm running an investigation and you're involved. I don't know just how much you're involved, but I intend to find out."

"You've got no right to question anyone, you've been suspended."

"I've been reinstated as of this morning. Now, sit down," I said sharply.

Wray looked at me as if he didn't quite believe me. He glanced at Martin, then sat down. He knew Martin was from Internal Affairs. If he was here, it had to be something serious.

"I've got a couple of questions for you. The first is why have you been following me?"

"God, you're paranoid," he said with a nervous laugh. "I haven't been following you."

"You drive a dark blue unmarked police car with the left front hubcap missing. You were outside my apartment, I've seen you outside Robin's apartment building, and I've seen you get in that car in the police garage."

"So what? That doesn't prove anything."

"So why have you been following me?"

"I haven't been following you."

"Okay, let's go onto something else. Who got you assigned to the lab? Remember, it's not that difficult for me to find out."

Wray looked at me, then at Martin. I could see that his mind was hard at work trying to figure out what to say. I also noticed that he glanced up at the one-way glass. I was sure he was wondering who might be behind it.

"I was assigned to help Kowalski in the lab by Lieutenant Brooks."

"Why? What did Brooks want you to do?"

Wray looked from me to Martin, then back at me. His anger at being here had subsided some. He was beginning to look more nervous than angry.

"Lieutenant Brooks wanted me to keep him informed on any evidence that turned up in the Robin Flower murder case."

"What were you supposed to do when something showed up?"

"I was to tell him about it, that's all."

"Are you sure that was all you were to do?"

"What do you mean?"

"Didn't Brooks want you to get rid of any incriminating evidence? Evidence that would link Tony or Brooks to the murder of Robin Flower?"

"I did no such thing. I did nothing more than tell him what evidence showed up. I have no idea what he did with the information after that."

"You did more than tell him about what evidence was found. You removed some evidence from the lab, didn't you?" I said.

"I did no such thing."

"You delivered a large yellow envelope to Joe Martonie in a small café just a few blocks from here. What was in the envelope?"

"I did no such thing," he answered nervously.

"Who was the envelope for?"

"I've had enough of this," he replied angrily, then stood up as if to leave.

"Sit down, Wray," Martin said in a commanding voice.

Wray looked at Sergeant Martin and hesitated for a second. The look on his face indicated that he was not sure what he should do now.

"I said, sit down," Martin repeated firmly.

Wray sat back down in the chair. He looked at me, then back at Martin. I could see the worried look on his face.

"You have the right to remain silent. Anything you say can and will be used against you in a court of law. You have a right to an attorney. If you can not afford one, one will be appointed before any further questioning," Martin said. "Do you understand what I'm telling you?"

Wray looked back at me. He looked as if he was beginning to understand the serious nature of the interrogation.

"Do you understand?" Martin said, demanding an answer.

"Yeah, I understand," Wray replied.

"Do you want a lawyer, Wray?" I asked after a long pause.

"No," he said softly.

"Don't you think it's about time to come clean? You're in about as much trouble as you can stand."

Wray had a long career with the department. As far as I knew he had been a good cop up until recently. I wondered what it was that made him turn into a bad cop.

"Okay," he said with a sigh.

"Do you know who killed Robin Flower?"

"I have no direct knowledge of who killed her."

"Do you have any indirect knowledge of who killed her?"

"Yes, and no."

"Which is it, yes or no?"

"Yes," he conceded.

"Tell me what you think you know."

"Will it go any easier on me?"

"I can't make that decision, but I will certainly put in a word for you provided what you tell me has some basis in fact."

Wray looked at me as if he was trying to decide what to tell me or how much to tell me. I got the feeling that he already knew that his career as a police officer was over.

About all he could do now would be to come clean and hope that he didn't end up in jail.

"There was a party at Frank Angelini's house. Robin went off to talk to Joe. It was innocent enough, but when Tony found out about it he flew into a rage. He immediately took Robin back to her apartment. At the apartment, or on the way to the apartment, she told Tony that she was not going to marry him. She also told him that she was in love with someone else.

"When she wouldn't tell Tony who she was having an affair with, he had Brooks hold her down while he shot her full of cocaine. I don't think he meant to give her as much as he did. I think he was trying to make her talk. Suddenly, she started convulsing and died."

"How do you know it was Brooks that held her down?"

"I guess I don't, really. All I know for sure is that Tony, Robin and Brooks left the party together. I saw them leave."

"Okay, go on."

"Tony went into a panic. It took awhile, but Brooks finally got him settled down enough to get him under control. He, Brooks, sent Tony back to the party and told him to tell his father that Robin was not feeling very well and had wanted to go home. He was to tell his father that since she was not feeling well, he had driven her home.

"After Tony left, Brooks called Charley Mitken to come to Robin's apartment and help him with a problem. I'm sure it was the two of them who arranged for Robin's body to be dumped on the beach at South Shore Park. Brooks called me to arrange for everyone to be in the park at the same time."

"Why did Brooks want all those people in the park?"

"He was trying to muddy the water and make things difficult for you. If he had you running every which way, you would not be able to pin it down to any one person. The longer you took to figure out who killed Robin, the more time he had to make sure that you didn't get too close to solving it. It would also give Brooks time to make any evidence that you found that pointed to Tony or himself disappear."

"How do you know all this?"

"Brooks told me about it over a few beers at his apartment."

"Why didn't you say anything about this before?"

Wray took a moment to look down at his hands folded in front of him on the table. He took a deep breath, looked up at me, then continued.

"Several years ago I took some money in exchange for looking the other way. Brooks found out about it and has been using it ever since."

"He's been blackmailing you?"

"Yeah. Every time he needed a favor, he called on me."

"Who shot Robin in the back of the head?"

"I don't know for sure, but you can bet it was Brooks."

"What makes you say that?"

"I saw him kill a drug dealer that same way about five years ago in an alley. You'll find that killing in your unsolved crimes file," Wray said with a note of authority.

"Why was Charley Mitken shot?"

"I don't know, but if I had to guess I would say it was to keep him quiet. He would have talked his head off if you had pressured him enough. He acted like a tough guy, but his biggest fear was going back to jail. That's what made him so valuable to Brooks, his fear of going back to jail."

"He's been in jail before, I wouldn't think it would be that big a thing to a thug like him."

"That's where you're wrong. Inside the joint, he's just a pawn. Out here, he's Mr. Tough Guy. All you'd have to do is threaten him with jail, and he'd squeal like a pig under an electric fence. I think Tony and Brooks knew that."

I looked over at Martin to see if he believed any of this. The look on his face gave me no indication of what he was thinking. I knew Wray's career was over, but so far I had done little to save mine.

"I guess I'm finished with you for now," I said as I pushed back in the chair to think.

I watched as Martin opened the door and motioned to someone. The next thing I knew, Wray was being taken into custody.

As soon as he was gone, Martin walked over to the table and sat down across from me. I looked up and let out a sigh.

My attention was directed to the one-way glass. I could hear a racket behind the glass. I could hear voices, but I could not tell what was being said. I wondered if Brooks had come unglued and confessed, but I was sure he would not break that easily.

I turned as the door opened and Captain Sinclair came into the interrogation room. He walked over to the table and sat down.

"I had Brooks taken down the hall to another room," Captain Sinclair said. "I was hoping that Wray would have gotten him to talk, but he denies everything Wray says. It looks like it will be Wray's word against Brooks."

"I'm still not off the hook, am I?"

"I'm afraid not. All you've got so far is 'hear say' evidence. That won't hold up in court. The evidence we have so far doesn't help you much," Martin said. "I'll be looking into the death of Danny Minger. So far, Wray is our prime suspect."

"Did your lab people find anything that will help?"

"I'm sorry, Nick. It's not looking good. Unless the lab turns up something that will help, you'll have to have a hearing," Captain Sinclair said.

Just then, there was a knock on the door. Martin stood up and answered the door. Jerry Kowalski stepped into the room with a large envelope, much like the one that I had seen Wray give to Joe Martonie.

"What have you got there, Jerry?" I asked.

"Just the pictures from inside the warehouse. I'm afraid they don't help much."

"Leave them here. I'd like to look at them," I said as I reached out for them.

"I've got some tire tracks that I'm trying to match up and some fingerprints, but that's about all. I wish I had better news for you."

"Thanks, Jerry," I said, thinking that my luck had better change fast if I was going to get out of this mess.

"Oh, by the way, there's a spot of blood that someone stepped in that shows up in one of the photos. I'm sorry, but there's not enough of an imprint to be able to tell who stepped in it," Jerry said.

"Thanks for trying," I said.

As Jerry left the interrogation room, Captain Sinclair stood up and leaned against the back of one of the chairs.

"Nick, we've still got Tony and Brooks to question. Maybe, we'll get something out of them."

I was sure that the captain was being overly optimistic, but I certainly had nothing left to lose at this point. If I could get one of them to say the wrong thing, I might be able to break this open.

"Okay. Let's take a go at Tony next. If we don't get anything out of him, we can question Brooks."

Captain Sinclair nodded and left the room. Martin followed along behind. I looked at the one-way glass that separated Monica from me. I smiled and winked, but I knew she would be able to see that I was worried.

CHAPTER TWENTY

While I was waiting for Tony, I sat looking at the pictures that Jerry Kowalski had given me. I came across the picture that showed the spot of blood that had been stepped in on the office floor in the warehouse. Another picture showed a close up of the same blood spot. On closer examination of the close up of the blood spot, I could see where a heel mark was made in the blood, but I couldn't see anything unusual about it. Before I had a chance to study it closely, Tony Angelini was escorted into the interrogation room.

An older man in an expensive tailored suit carrying a brown leather briefcase followed Tony into the interrogation room. Tony sat down at the end of the table and the man sat down beside him.

"I see you've brought counsel, Tony," I said.

"I'm J. P. Casini, attorney at law. I represent Mr. Anthony Angelini."

"I'm Detective Nicholas McCord, and the gentleman standing against the wall is Sergeant Bill Martin of Internal Affairs. We have already given your client his rights," I said. "Would you like us to repeat them in your presence?"

"That won't be necessary."

"Fine, then let's get on with it."

"Before he answers any questions, I have two questions to ask you. First of all, what does Internal Affairs have to do with this?"

"We believe that there is a least one police officer, possibly two that are involved in the case we are investigating. That is the reason that Sergeant Martin is working with me."

"Second, I want to know what Mr. Angelini is being charged with?"

"At this point, we are not charging him with anything. However, it does look like we may be charging Mr. Angelini with the murder of Miss Robin Flower."

I watched Tony for any change in his expression. I noticed a little tightening of his neck muscles, but that was all. He was nervous, and I was sure he had every right to be.

"I, of course, will not allow my client to answer any questions that I deem to be not in his best interest," Mr. Casini said with an air of arrogance.

"Of course," I replied, then turned to Tony.

"Did you take Robin to her apartment on the night before she was found dead on the beach?"

"Yes," Tony replied after he looked to his lawyer for direction.

"Was Lieutenant Brooks in her apartment with you at that time?"

Again, he looked to his lawyer before answering.

"Yes."

"Did you give Robin a shot of cocaine?"

"I don't think my client will answer that question," Mr. Casini said before Tony had a chance to say anything.

I got the feeling that this was going to be a long afternoon. If he was not going to answer my questions, I was sure that I would get little out of him. I needed answers if I was to save my own skin. I decided to take a little different approach.

"You had Brooks deliver a message to me that you wanted to see me at your warehouse. Is that correct?"

"Yes."

"Brooks was in the warehouse along with several of your personal bodyguards. Is that correct?"

"Yes."

"You had Charley Mitken brought into the warehouse office and had Lieutenant Brooks shoot him in the back of the head with my gun. Didn't you?"

"My client will not answer that. I think you better go fishing some place else, and that's all this is. You have no proof that my client was even in that warehouse at the time, or even shortly after Charley Mitken was shot."

"That's where you're wrong. By the way, I can prove it."

Tony looked from me to his attorney, then back at me. I could see that for the first time, he was feeling really scared. For the first time, he was not sure that he would be getting out of this mess.

I reached out and picked up one of the pictures. I pushed it across the table in front of Tony. I knew I was bluffing, but I couldn't think of anything else that would make him talk.

"Take a real good look at that picture. The picture was taken in your warehouse. If you look close enough, you'll notice a couple of spots of blood on the floor. It is Charley Mitken's blood. The one on the left, near the corner of the desk, is not clear. A blow up of that part of the picture shows that the blood was stepped in. Left in the blood was a very clear print of the heel of a very expensive Italian shoe. Your shoe, Tony. We have you at the scene of the murder of Charley Mitken."

Tony turned pale and gasped for air. I could see the sweat begin to roll down his temples.

"You want to talk to me now?"

"I think my client has said all he's going to say for now," the attorney said as he stood up.

"Well, Tony? You're going down for two murders. Robin Flowers' and Charley Mitken's?"

"No. I didn't murder Mitken," he yelled out.

"Don't say another word," Casini said as he tried to shut up Tony.

"I'm not taking the blame for both. Brooks killed Mitken," Tony cried out.

"Shut up, you damn fool," Casini yelled.

Just then, I heard something smack up against the one-way glass. I could hear voices from behind the glass, but was unable to tell what was being said or what was happening. It sounded like there was a scuffle going on.

The sounds stopped as quickly as they had begun. I couldn't be sure, but I had a good feeling run through me. I was sure that Tony had said enough to cause Brooks to come unglued. I was sure that if Brooks could have gotten to me, he would like nothing more than to kill me, and undoubtedly Tony.

"Tony Angelini, you are under arrest for the murder of Robin Flower, and as an accessory to the murder of Charley Mitken. Martin, take him away."

"You get me out of here," Tony yelled at his attorney.

"Sorry, Tony. There's no bail for the charge of first degree murder," I said as Martin put handcuffs on him and led him out the door to the jail.

Tony's attorney followed them out the door leaving me alone. I slouched back in the chair and let out a sigh of relief. It was over. There would be a hearing to see if I had broken any regulations or policies by going to the warehouse alone, but that would be it.

Suddenly, the door flew open and Monica rushed in. There was a smile on her face and tears running down her cheeks. I no more then got to my feet when she threw her arms around my neck and kissed me. I heard the door behind us open again, but I didn't want to let go of her.

"Excuse me," Captain Sinclair said, a big grin across his face.

"Yes, sir, I replied as Monica took her arms from around my neck and moved to my side.

"I guess you're off the hook. Brooks came apart when Tony said that he had killed Mitken. He said that Tony killed Robin. When you are through here, would you mind coming to my office," he said with a smile, then left the room.

As soon as the door closed, Monica turned to me again. I slipped my arms around her and held her close. I knew that she was all that was important to me.

After we kissed for several minutes, we sat down at the table. I just sat there looking at her and holding her hand. She was so beautiful.

"What are you thinking?"

"I'm thinking that I should take you back to the apartment. I need to get a few things cleared up here, then we can spend the rest of the night together."

"Okay, but I can get a cab. You get done here and I'll meet you at the apartment."

"Great."

I walked her out to the front desk and talked with the sergeant on duty. He was kind enough to arrange for an officer to take Monica to my apartment.

As soon as she was gone, I went up to Captain Sinclair's office. He wasn't there, so I sat down on the sofa to wait.

Captain Sinclair came back in about an hour. I was still sitting on the sofa, my head tipped back and my eyes closed. I could not explain the feeling of relief that had come over me now that I had been cleared of killing Charley Mitken.

"I'm glad you stuck around," he said.

"What's happening?"

"Tony is talking his head off. It seems that Wray was right. Tony, in a jealous rage, had Brooks hold Robin down while he shot her full of cocaine. The problem came when he used too much. Robin went into convulsions and died.

"Brooks got Tony out of there, sending him back to the party. He then shot Robin in the back of the head in the hope that someone would think she was killed by someone trying to get at the Angelini family."

"Surely, Brooks would know that we would quickly discover that she died of an overdose of drugs?"

"Sure. All he was interested in doing was causing so much confusion that it would be almost impossible to prove any theory you came up with was the right one. It would give him time to figure out what evidence to use and what to make disappear, with Wray's help.

"The reason for providing you with so many suspects was the same, to keep you so busy trying to sort out who was involved and who wasn't that you couldn't settle in on a single motive."

"Did Tony point the finger directly at Brooks for the murder of Charley?"

"He not only pointed the finger at Brooks, but said he would provide witnesses if I would deal with him."

"Did you agree?"

"No. I leave that to the DA."

"Now what?"

"I think you should go home and spend some time away from here. If I had a woman like Miss Barnhart waiting for me, I wouldn't spend one minute longer around here than necessary."

"I'll see you tomorrow," I said as I stood up.

"Nick, why don't you make it in a couple of days," he said with a smile.

I didn't have to be told twice. I was up off that sofa and out of the police station before he could change his mind.

When I arrived back at the apartment, I found Monica waiting at the door. She threw her arms around me and held me. As I wrapped my arms around her, we kissed and kissed. It was a homecoming like I had never had before.

"I have dinner ready for you," she said as she looked up at me.

"Sounds great. I didn't realize how hungry I was until just a few minutes ago."

We went to the kitchen and ate. We didn't talk much. After dinner, we left the dirty dishes on the counter and walked to the bedroom.

"I'm going to take a shower," I said.

"I'm not letting you out of my sight," she said with a smile.

We went to the bathroom together. It didn't take us long to get our clothes off and get into the shower. The feel of her body pressing against me as I ran my hands over her drove our desire for each other beyond belief. Our need for each other only continued when we finally got into bed.

We missed the performance of Phantom of the Opera, but it didn't matter. Tonight had been our night to be together, and nothing would take it away from us.

CPSIA information can be obtained
at www.ICGtesting.com
Printed in the USA
LVHW080739150721
692757LV00010B/761